W9-CQB-187

rossini

compact companions

PHILIPS *Classics*

<small>COMPACT COMPANIONS</small>

ROSSINI

<small>DAVID MOUNTFIELD</small>

<small>**SIMON & SCHUSTER**</small>

<small>NEW YORK LONDON TORONTO SYDNEY TOKYO SINGAPORE</small>

SIMON & SCHUSTER
ROCKEFELLER CENTER
1230 AVENUE OF THE AMERICAS
NEW YORK, NEW YORK 10020

Designed by Wherefore Art? Edited by Emma Lawson.

Printed and bound in Singapore by Imago Publishing Ltd.
10 9 8 7 6 5 4 3 2 1

Library of Congress Cataloging-in-Publication Data
Mountfield, David, 1938-
Rossini / David Mountfield.
p.   cm.   —   (Compact companions)
Discography: p.
Includes bibliographical references (p.   ).
ISBN 0-684-81361-0
1. Rossini, Gioacchino, 1792–1868. 2. Composers—Italy—Biography. I. Series.
ML410. R8M68 1995
782. 1'092—dc20
[B]   95-5611
CIP
MN

Front cover picture reproduced by kind permission of AKG and the Mansell Collection

Contents

Monsieur D'Ageus

Danton fit jadis la Caricature du Cor posseur Paganese
Aujourd'hui devenu Pianiste de la quatrième Classe il ne
s'oppose pas à ce qu'elle soit Publiée dans votre Journal

G. Rossini

Passy 28 Juin 1867

A caricature of Rossini by Mailly, 1867 (Lebrecht)

Musical Heritage

In spite of stories of his 'apprenticeship' to a blacksmith, or a Bologna sausage maker, there was never much doubt that Gioachino Antonio Rossini would be a musician. Not only was his father a professional horn player and his mother a singer of some local fame, but Gioachino himself, as is so often the way with a musical genius, manifested his own ability very early in life. He first appeared on the operatic stage while still a natural treble, and the excellence of his unbroken voice is said to have prompted the suggestion, vetoed by his mother, that he should submit to the operation required to become a castrato. This was Rossini's story in later life, though it is slightly suspect since, by the early nineteenth century, castratos were beginning to go out of style. Moreover, Rossini's strong sense of humor inclined him to adorn accounts of his early life with the odd cadenza. He was himself largely responsible for becoming, as his first English biographer, Francis Toye, said, 'the subject of more spurious anecdotes [and] the father, real or putative, of more jokes than any other musician'.

Rossini's parents – he was their only child – were certainly musicians, but not quite in the sense suggested by, say, a first violinist in the Philharmonic or a member of the chorus at La Scala. His mother, according to him, could not read a note of music and had to learn her parts by ear, while his father, although he may have received a musical training of some sort and came from a family rumored to have been of greater social account in earlier generations, could read and write only with difficulty. They were roving musicians, of a sort not very common nowadays even in the pop world, but not unusual in eighteenth-century Italy. Giuseppe Rossini was in effect a jobbing tradesman, prepared to move from place to place in search of work.

When the future composer was born, on February 29, 1792, the family lived in Pesaro, in the region known as the Marches, on the coast between Rimini and Ancona. Now largely given over to vacationers, 200 years ago it was an unpretentious fishing port, and the old town still retains much historic charm. When Rossini was born there, in a two-room apartment in a street now named after him, Pesaro was situated within the Papal States, one of the many political units into which Italy was then divided. The effects of French conquests and the rise of liberalism and nationalism were to bring tumultuous changes during Rossini's youth. Neither he nor anyone else could be immune to the effects of such changes, but beyond that they had no great effect on Rossini personally: his interest in political affairs was never more than superficial. He was no great republican like his father, and his alleged lack of patriotism in later years, when the revolutionary, Giuseppe Mazzini, was fomenting Italian nationalism, was to cause almost the only blight on his popularity among his fellow countrymen.

His father held the post of town trumpeter – equivalent to town crier – in Pesaro, which, if not very well paid, at least provided regular and not too demanding employment. During the season, he also played in the orchestra at the opera house, and he further augmented his income by playing at weddings and other parties.

Giuseppe was thirty-two when he married the twenty-year-old Anna Guidarini. She was a daughter of the house where he had lodgings, and earned some sort of a living through needlework. It appears to have been an easy-going household. As

Rossini's father, Giuseppe
(Lebrecht)

*Rossini's mother, Anna
(Lebrecht)*

their son was born only five months afterwards, the marriage, in the old (it has since been largely rebuilt) cathedral of the Annunciation in Pesaro, may not have been entirely voluntary. Nevertheless, it seems to have worked well; relations between the son and both parents remained close and loving.

From what we know of him, Giuseppe Rossini appears as a slightly cruder version of his son, and as a character who might almost have come out of the *opera buffa* tradition himself. In Pesaro he gained the nickname 'Vivazza', and he possessed in abundance those familiar qualities of energy and enthusiasm. His natural exuberance was to be passed on to his son.

During the 1790s, when power changed hands several times between the papal authorities, backed by Austria and the French, Giuseppe's republican sympathies got him into trouble, on one occasion into jail. The political situation settled down somewhat after 1800, when Napoleon Bonaparte, having established his authority in France, invaded Italy, destroyed the Austrian army at Marengo, and re-established French control, which was eventually extended to virtually all of Italy.

Meanwhile, the Rossinis had embarked upon an itinerant existence in search of work, with Giuseppe encouraging Anna to exploit her fine natural soprano. Under the reactionary administration of the papal authorities, women were forbidden to appear on stage, although the rule was frequently infringed. This partly accounted for the popularity of the castrati, though it was not the only reason. Rossini himself paid tribute to 'the purity, the wonderful flexibility of those voices and, above all, their deeply penetrating quality', and he wrote a part for one of the last of them, Giovanni Battista Velluti, in his *Aureliano in Palmira* (1813).

For a few years Anna was possibly the chief breadwinner. It was her career that drew them on their travels around the small opera houses, with Giuseppe usually managing to get work in the orchestra. The greatest success in Anna's rather short, six-year career as a singer was a season in 1802 in Trieste, where she appeared with, and rivaled, a famous contemporary contralto and courtesan, Giuseppina Grassini, who was said to have included Napoleon among her former lovers.

The young Gioachino was with his parents in Trieste, but in general it was impractical for him to accompany them, and he was entrusted to the care of his mother's family in Pesaro. He was a handful, hard to control, less than keen on school, and given to fairly serious pranks, such as raiding the church sacristy. The intervals he spent with a blacksmith and a butcher were efforts to curb his unruliness.

In 1802 the family left Pesaro and moved to Lugo, east of Bologna, Giuseppe Rossini's home town. Their house in Lugo was eventually inherited by the composer, who could not bring himself to sell it though he never lived there again.

In Lugo, at the house of the well-to-do and musical Malerbi family, the ten-year-old Rossini encountered a rather different musical tradition, that represented in particular by Haydn and by Mozart; he was to describe Mozart in a well-judged phrase in later years as 'the admiration of my youth, the desperation of my mature years, and the consolation of my old age'. Like most other non-German composers of the nineteenth century, Rossini was to encounter occasional criticism, especially from fervent nationalists, that his music was 'too German'. (Others, of course, thought he was not German enough.)

In the Malerbi household Rossini also learned something of composition. In 1804, when he was twelve years old, quite elderly by Mozart's standard, he composed some pieces for a rich neighbor, Agostino Triossi, which featured along

Rossini's birthplace: Pesaro in Italy (Mansell)

Padre Stanislao Mattei,
Rossini's first tutor (Lebrecht)

with his cousins and Rossini himself (second violin) in the string quartet that gave them their first performance. As an adult, confronted with this early work, Rossini was condemnatory, yet others would say that it already possessed some of the qualities for which his mature music was to be celebrated, such as a lively spontaneity and cheerful ease of expression.

At about this time his mother's professional singing career came to an end: she had often suffered from throat trouble and it is surprising that, in view also of her lack of training in the demanding tradition of the Italian opera, her voice had lasted so long. Her son, however, was already contributing to the family income. In fact there is a record of him being paid a small sum in Pesaro at the age of six, apparently for playing a small percussion instrument, and he had been singing in churches and elsewhere for several years.

Lugo, like Pesaro, was a small town and, in search of greater opportunities and perhaps of better education for Gioachino, the family moved to Bologna in 1804. Not only was Bologna a substantial city, it had a reputation as a musical center, not so much for opera as for more serious musical studies. It contained the Accademia Filarmonica, a seventeenth-century foundation of international reputation, as well as the more recent Liceo Musicale, an offshoot of the Accademia, which was run by Padre Stanislao Mattei. Rossini studied singing as well as cello, harpsichord and counterpoint, the last with Mattei.

In some respects the conservative Mattei was an unlikely tutor for such as Rossini – and, a few years later, Donizetti. Although Rossini's studies at the Liceo continued for six years, they were increasingly irregular, and in 1810, when Mattei advised him that he faced two more years on fugue, plainsong and canon, he declared he had done enough, though according to one report, financial considerations may have had something to do with his departure. He was still more interested in Haydn and, especially, Mozart who, incidentally, had been elected a member of the Accademia Filarmonica at fourteen, the same age as Rossini.

He made other useful musical contacts in Bologna, among them the Mombelli family, who included Domenico, a famous tenor, and his daughters Anna and Ester, about Rossini's age, who were to develop into soprano and contralto respectively.

Rossini in his sixties told how he first became intimate with Domenico Mombelli; the episode also illustrates his remarkable musical memory. He was asked by a lady friend – he implied an amorous connection and though he was only thirteen at the time that possibility cannot be discounted – to obtain a copy of an aria in the possession of the Mombelli family. At that time singers often had their own, so-called 'suitcase arias', jealously guarded and performed when opportunity arose, often on quite inappropriate occasions; in fact, most of Rossini's early vocal compositions were pieces of this sort. Mombelli and his copyist both declined to provide a copy of the aria, so Rossini declared that he would attend the next performance and afterwards write it down from memory. This he did (a similar story, of which Rossini was no doubt aware, is told of Mozart), and Mombelli was so impressed that he asked Rossini to set some pieces written by his wife. This was the origin of Rossini's first opera, *Demetrio e Polibio*, at least his first-written opera – it was written by 1808 though not performed until 1812, when the Mombelli girls were old enough to sing it.

Rossini himself sang in a production of an opera by his contempory and fellow Italian Ferdinando Paër in 1805 and in a concert by the students of the Liceo in the following year, but that was his swansong as a boy soprano.

He was maturing in every way. In one scene in Paër's opera he was called upon to cast himself upon the bosom of the *prima donna*. This was one of two different ladies, playing alternate performances. One possessed the sort of bosom that a precocious youth would enjoy casting himself upon, the other did not. This fact, it is said, was reflected in Rossini's performance of the scene.

His voice subsequently developed into what is usually described as a tenor-baritone, but continued a useful instrument. In later years he was to 'sing for his supper' at grand parties in many European cities.

He continued to compose, including an overture in D major for his patron Agostino Triossi and several duets for horns, an instrument of which he remained fond, no doubt because he had first learned to play it at his father's knee. His cantata *Orfeo* followed in 1808.

Meanwhile, though he could no longer earn fees by singing, he was gaining important practical experience, as well as money, at various minor opera houses where he was employed as a *répétiteur*, playing at rehearsals and coaching the singers. At an early age, and in a sense throughout his career, he was a jobbing musician like his father, if on a more elevated plain.

Rossini never regarded himself as one of the great masters; he was no Mozart and he knew it. Few eminent composers have managed to retain such a practical, down-to-earth attitude towards their work, and his modesty – he was more vain about his appearance than his compositions – is one of his most attractive characteristics. On the other hand, it sometimes invited, and still invites, the scorn of those to whom musical composition should be a matter of blood, sweat and tears.

That is not to suggest a lack of firm principles or opinions. For instance, Rossini provided early evidence of his dislike of the still-current fashion for singers to embroider their parts with often absurdly extravagant cadenzas and other coloratura effects (in his own operas he was to eliminate this custom by writing his own vocal decorations). At the age of fourteen he got into trouble when he reacted to a particularly unworkable effort by a well-known soprano, Adelaide Carpano, with laughter. She complained to her patron, a rich and aristocratic Venetian impresario, the Marchese Cavalli, who responded with fierce threats but, after Rossini had explained things, he changed his attitude. Impressed by the young man's abilities, he told Rossini that if or when he ever came to write an opera himself he would be interested to see it. This was to prove no idle promise. Moreover, Adelaide Carpano was to sing Zaida at the first performance of Rossini's *Il turco in Italia* (1814).

La Carpano was also, no doubt, the Marchese's mistress: the time when singers were regarded as little different from whores was passing, but the contemporary equivalent of the studio couch was certainly influential, and in the world of the Italian opera, sex tended to be more rampant than normal. Cavalli himself had some reputation for enforcing his *droit de seigneur*, and Rossini was no slouch in this area, though perhaps less prodigious than, in later years, he liked to suggest. He was to suffer for it. His poor health in later life was probably due to a venereal disease, an affliction which was to destroy Donizetti.

At about this time Rossini first met, or at any rate saw and heard, a greater singer, who was to play an important part in his life. This was Isabella Colbran, the Spanish soprano and the greatest dramatic coloratura of her time. She made her debut in Paris in 1801, when she was sixteen (seven years older than Rossini), and

*Isabella Colbran,
singer, the
composer's long-
term mistress, and
first wife
(Mansell)*

came to Bologna on being elected to the Accademia Filarmonica in 1806. After several performances in Bologna, she left for Milan, where she was to make her debut at La Scala. Apart from her voice, which won the highest acclaim from her contemporaries, she had powerful physical presence and classical good looks: 'beauty in the most regal tradition, noble features which on stage radiated majesty, an eye like that of a Circassian maid, flashing fire'. That was Stendhal's judgment, though he added waspishly that 'off stage she had about as much dignity as the average milliner's assistant'.

Among the acquaintances of the Rossinis were a couple named Morandi, who had worked with them at various opera houses. In 1810 they stopped over in Bologna on their way to Venice, where they had been engaged by the Marchese Cavalli at the Teatro San Moisè. They promised to look out for any opportunities in Venice for the young Rossini.

Arriving there, they found that Cavalli, having contracted to produce a number of new *farse* (one-act *opera buffa*), had been let down by one of his composers. The Morandis mentioned Rossini, Cavalli remembered being impressed by him, and summoned him to Venice.

Venice, when Rossini first arrived there, retained but a shadow of its former greatness. Its commercial eminence had been fading since the Renaissance, and Napoleon had delivered the final blow to the ancient republic when he invaded in 1797 and threw out the doge and the senators, remarking ominously that he would be Venice's Atilla. The glittering empire was now fast declining into what it remains, an attractive museum piece, dependent largely on tourists. In the world of music, Venice could no longer boast of famous composers, not living ones that is,

Piazza di San Marco, Venice, painted by Roberto Roberti in 1810 (AKG)

and the former heart of the Italian opera, site of one of the first public opera houses, was fast being overtaken by Milan and Naples.

On the other hand, the fading of Venice's grandeur had not reduced her people to gloom and despondency. They continued to celebrate life and culture with their traditional panache. They had not lost their love for the theater or for opera, and in that respect the prestige of Venice remained high. Three flourishing opera houses survived, as well as several other theaters.

It was normal practice for the composer to be presented with a libretto, and on his arrival a revamped libretto called *La cambiale di matrimonio* was hastily thrust upon Rossini, which he was required to set in a few days. The score was not at first seen as entirely satisfactory, some of the singers complaining about what they were asked to sing. Morandi, himself a competent composer, sorted out the difficulties, and the work appeared in a double bill at the Teatro San Moisè in November. Though the composer was only eighteen, most critics agree that *La cambiale* – melodious, brisk, unsentimental, with a clear eye for musical realization of the ridiculous – shows him already in command of the gifts which were soon to make him famous. It was a success. Moreover, Rossini received what seemed to him at that time a substantially high fee, and as the family must have been hard up, that was almost as satisfactory as the plaudits.

Rossini returned to Bologna, where, perhaps as a result of his success in Venice, he was commissioned to write a two-act opera for the Teatro del Corso, *L'equivoco stravagante*, in which an aspiring lover outmaneuvers a rival by persuading him that the girl they both desire is actually a castrato in disguise. It was produced in October 1811. Accounts of its reception vary, but unfortunately it fell foul of the censors, and had to be taken off after only three performances.

This disappointment was soon forgotten as, within a few weeks, Rossini was back in Venice, where he had been asked to write another *farsa* for the San Moisè. This was *L'inganno felice*, which was as well received as its predecessor, playing right through to the end of the season.

Working with the speed for which he was to become famous, Rossini was in Ferrara in March to present his first (or first-performed) *opera seria*, *Ciro in Babilonia*. It was possible to circumvent the rule against opera in Lent by basing it on the Bible and calling it an 'oratorio'. However, *Ciro* was a hiccup in Rossini's fast-blossoming career; he later described it himself as 'one of my fiascos'. It is chiefly well known for containing the famous aria in which all the work is done by the orchestra and the singer has to sing only one note – B♭ – as Rossini had discovered that was the only note this lady could sing without sounding dreadful.

At the San Moisè in Venice, however, they were anxious for Rossini to repeat his success with *L'inganno* and he had already agreed to write another farsa before the calamity of *Ciro*. *La scala di seta* (1812), though quite well received, was something of a disappointment. The libretto was of more than average banality, and though it has an overture that flows like a river, the opera has seldom been performed since Rossini's time. A story that the composer was so annoyed by the libretto he was given to set that he deliberately sabotaged the work by writing music inappropriate to the circumstances of a particular scene seems to be without foundation. The same story is also told of next year's San Moisè offering, *Il signor Bruschino*, but neither music nor libretto offers any supporting evidence.

No setback to Rossini's career ensued from the tepid reception of *L'inganno*. In

Bologna, again through the influence of singers he had previously worked with, he received a commission from La Scala, Milan, for a two-act opera. Not only was the fee more than double what he received in Venice, a success at La Scala would underline the promise he had already shown and lead to more and bigger contracts. Fortunately, *La pietra del paragone* was greeted ecstatically when it opened in September 1812 and repeated a remarkable fifty-three times in the course of the season. It so impressed the French regent in Milan that he used his influence to have Rossini released from the tiresome obligation of military service, for which he was now eligible (Donizetti, later, was also able to work this trick).

In Milan in 1812, Rossini must have renewed his acquaintance with Isabella Colbran. Around the same time, the work that Rossini had written at the age of about sixteen for the Mombellis, without knowing that it would become an opera, was performed by them in Rome. Apparently, Rossini was not present; he later said that Mombelli had not told him of the forthcoming production.

As anticipated, more offers followed La Scala's. Once more, Venice summoned him, but this time, besides the San Moisè, the most distinguished of Venetian opera houses, La Fenice, wanted Rossini, and his work for that famous theater was to establish beyond question his reputation as the outstanding young composer in Italy.

That standing was no doubt reinforced by the relative lack of competition at this time. Neither Donizetti nor Bellini were yet underway. Of the older generation, the most distinguished, Cimarosa, had died in 1801. His nearest rival, Paisiello, was in his seventies and had composed little for several years.

Cherubini and Spontini had become French. Rossini's active contemporaries included competent people like Paër and the German-born Simon Mayr, but no one of anything like Rossini's talent. It was time for promise to mature into achievement.

Gaetano Donizetti painted in 1835 by Pasinetti (AKG)

Italian Opera

To the average passenger on the 6:03 from London, the word 'music' probably summons up, first and foremost, the German symphonic tradition, but to the equivalent citizen taking his seat on the stage coach at the Bull and Mouth 200 years ago, it meant Italian opera.

True opera began in Italy about 1600. Of course, it can be traced further, through the medieval mystery plays and back to Greek drama; in fact, the pioneers of opera in Florence and Rome were trying to get back to those distant – and really unknowable – classical roots.

The earliest operas would attract few *aficionados* today: they consisted of almost continual recitative, with a skimpy score and not much in the way of an orchestra. Monteverdi is the first great figure: he was largely responsible for moving opera out of the princely courts to which it was first confined and into public theaters: Florence, the birthplace of opera, also had the first public opera house, in 1657. The subject matter was invariably drawn from history and myth, and the chief attraction of opera was probably the scenery and elaborate stage effects. The English diarist John Evelyn, in Venice in 1645, was amazed by the 'variety of sceanes painted and contrived with no lesse art of perspective, and machines for flying in the aire, and other wonderful motions' – and all this for a ticket price of two lire.

French opera was not established until the late seventeenth century, and Italian influence in Paris was strong right from the start. Even Lully, though thoroughly French, was actually of Italian birth. Seventeenth-century French opera contained much ballet, as Louis XIV was fond of it, and it was probably in France that the decisive separation of recitative and aria took place. The custom of accompanying the recitative with strings, rather than harpsichord continuo, is also said by some authorities to have developed in France.

In England also, opera seemed to have made a promising beginning with Purcell; unfortunately, he proved to be both the beginning and the end of the tradition in the seventeenth century. More important was his Italian contemporary, Scarlatti, whose popularity finally overcame the opposition of the Church. Scarlatti introduced more dramatic expression as well as the *da capo* (first part repeated) aria. In general, though, Scarlatti operated within the rigid conventions by which the Italian opera was already defined. Opera has always been remarkably successful at getting away with the totally improbable because it is part of the convention, and never more than in the days when the mighty figure of some bearded Greek god or hero strode the stage defying the Fates or the Persians in a thrilling soprano.

Italian opera was also popular in Germany, and the young Handel had spent several years in Italy before he settled in England and delighted the English with thirty-five works in the Italian style, works full of glorious music, consisting predominantly of arias and thoroughly non-dramatic – as well as fiendishly hard on the singers.

The standard form was the *opera seria*, formal, complex, with highly ornamental arias allotted to the singers according to formula – the *prima donna* getting more than the *seconda donna*. Popular taste demanded more and more arias, to the disgust of the more sophisticated connoisseurs, and a *prima donna* also had to have arias in different styles or moods, to display her virtuosity. Though 'serious', these works usually had a happy ending, Italian audiences being known to complain that a tragic ending put them off their supper.

Undoubtedly, eighteenth-century opera was a rigid and increasingly stagnant art form and, as so often happens, the form having reached its peak, decadence set in. Mozart's *Idomeneo* (1781) was almost the last traditional *opera seria* of real distinction. The Italian opera was reinvigorated by the rise of the *opera buffa*, 'comic opera', to which Rossini was to make so substantial a contribution.

In search of humor and popular appeal, *opera buffa* forsook those over-exploited mythological tales and took its subject matter and its characters – such as the barber of Seville – from everyday life, facilitating audience identification. Like most supposed innovations in the arts, this was not entirely new: operas including peasants and dialect had been produced a century earlier, though no real tradition was established until the custom arose of inserting a *buffo* act in between the acts of an *opera seria*, with no relation between the two.

In France arguments arose between the partisans of *opera buffa* and the French *opéra-comique* (rather a slippery term historically, but characterized by spoken dialogue). This was not the first nor the last conflict between the native and the Italian traditions in France. In Rossini's time, it took the form of rivalry between the Paris Opéra and the Théâtre-Italien, the latter being much the livelier place at least until the 1830s.

Meanwhile, in the late eighteenth century, the finest Italian operas so far had been written by an Austrian. Mozart's earliest operas belonged to the German *Singspiel* tradition, closer to what today would be called a musical [play]. With *Le nozze di Figaro* (1786) he produced a superb example of the *opera buffa*, and continued

The 28-year-old Rossini. He had already written Barber of Seville, Mosè in Egitto *and* Otello
(AKG)

in the Italian comic tradition with *Don Giovanni* (1787) and *Così fan tutte* (1790).

As in other respects, Mozart is *sui generis*. His is a more human form of *opera buffa*. The characters are not, as they tend to be in others, mere clowns, and there are serious elements as well as farce. He had no significant followers in German opera, which was to be thrown out of its stride by the Italian resurgence represented by Rossini with reinforcements from Bellini and Donizetti. Beethoven wrote only one opera (some would say the best, however), while Schubert, incomparable composer of songs, wrote none (though he did write musical stage works), and Meyerbeer felt compelled to move to Italy (later Paris). Weber was a partial exception, and kept the fire going for the coming Wagnerian explosion, but he failed to dislodge the Italian opera from its favored place among German, and particularly Viennese, audiences.

However, the long ascendancy of Italy in music generally seemed – or can now be seen – to be ending towards the end of the eighteenth century. Even the ascendancy of the Italian opera seemed to be in doubt. The main trouble was a lack of talent. Cimarosa was almost the only worthwhile practitioner. Cherubini was better – Haydn regarded him as the best living composer, bar himself – but Cherubini had gone to France, where he wrote French operas. Spontini also forsook his native land for the more challenging environment of Paris in 1804. There, Napoleon suggested the subject of his *Fernand Cortez* (1809), the first Italian production of which was to be conducted by Rossini a decade later. However, the golden age of French grand opera was not quite dawning yet. When it did, some twenty years later, Rossini, strangely enough, was a major contributor, with his *Guillaume Tell* (1829).

What Rossini did for French opera, however, was nothing compared with what he did for Italian opera. Not only Rossini: a new generation was born in the final decade of the eighteenth century, which included Rossini, Donizetti and Bellini, as well as several others of rather less talent.

These three were to restore the fortunes of Italian opera and reinforce its international appeal, which extended to every European country, and to the Americas. No other tradition could make any headway against it outside its own country of origin. The largest theater in London, the King's Theatre, Haymarket, for which Handel had formerly written (its present successor, Her Majesty's, occupies a portion of the site) functioned for years on a diet of constant Rossini with a few injections of Mozart.

Italians love singing. Foreign travelers in the nineteenth century often remarked upon the fact, which is still evident today in the back streets of a city such as Naples. To attempt to analyze the Italian gift for song would be otiose, but as Stendhal remarked, a young man in Italy would write a song as easily as a young man in France would write a letter, and the importance of opera in the cultural life of the several disparate political divisions of Italy when Rossini was young would be hard to exaggerate. It is said that there were some two hundred opera houses in the country. Big cities had several, and a town of any size would feel depressed and deprived without one.

Moreover, these theaters were generally very grand buildings; large too, for they incorporated much more than a simple auditorium. The spacious gambling salons at La Scala were, in economic terms, of greater significance than the opera, and when they were abolished people feared the theater would be ruined.

During the season at least, the opera house vied with the church as the central institution of the town. The first night was *the* night of the year. Theaters were used for a great variety of festivities besides opera, and even for state occasions: the Teatro San Carlo in Naples was virtually a branch of the royal government; when it burned down in 1816 it was rebuilt with a speed that would astonish our cultural bureaucrats today.

The carnival season was the season for opera, although in larger places, with two or more opera houses, it extended to most of the year except for Lent and high summer – and as time went by it encroached steadily on these periods too. The importance of the opera as a cultural focal point was perhaps even more significant in smaller towns: the nearest modern equivalent is a professional football team. Enthusiasm was intense, and so was criticism. The impresario, usually a rich man who lived locally, attracted the same kind of attention as the modern Wall Street trader though, since he was often a figure of some social status, possibly more respectful. The lives and characters of those he recruited from various places as his 'staff' – librettist, composer (usually in that order), singers – came under close and critical scrutiny and, as rehearsals got under way, there was generally no shortage of scandalous liaisons to keep the gossips busy.

The extraordinary importance of opera in the lives of ordinary people cannot be ascribed solely to the Italians' love of music – although that motive should not be disregarded. The fact was that life in Italy was rather dull, dull in the same sort of way as it was more recently in eastern European countries under the deadening rule of communism. Repressive political and religious powers discouraged any kind of original thinking on almost any subject. It has even been suggested that these powers encouraged opera because it did not stimulate mental activity. However, to

La Scala, Milan painted in 1852 by Angelo Inganni (AKG)

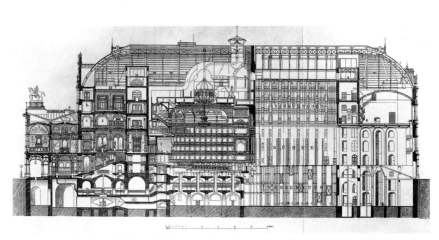

A cross-section of the Vienna State Opera, revealing the layout of a typical theater or opera house (AKG)

be on the safe side, strict rules governed the opera houses; censorship was weighty and thorough. In Rome, it was necessary to submit forty copies of a libretto to various censors, lay and ecclesiastical, before performance could be licensed.

Certainly, Italian audiences wanted amiable and entertaining music, music that was easily digested ('like a plate of macaroni', Berlioz scathingly remarked), music that made no great demands on the listener, indeed, as one irritated foreigner complained, that did not have to be listened to.

All accounts agree that Italian audiences were markedly inattentive. They commonly talked loudly throughout the recitative and only shut up for the arias, if then. Sometimes they would listen to their favorite singer and take up other amusements, such as flirting or playing cards, eating and drinking, or catching up on their sleep, when others held the stage. Theaters consisted of a pit, the 'orchestra' or stalls, with tiers of galleries made up of boxes, usually privately owned or rented out. Within these boxes practically anything could go on, and as they had curtains which could be drawn to conceal the occupants, practically anything no doubt did.

To be fair, people had an excuse for this behavior. Because the opera was essentially a social institution, people did not go there once or twice, as they would now, they went nearly every night. A large proportion of a given audience might be seeing the same work for the tenth time, when full attention would be hard to maintain. In Milan, evening parties were seldom given on any day except Friday, because that was the night La Scala was closed. Otherwise, everybody who was anybody was at the opera.

Many operas were intended for one production only, and many received no more. To the advantage of the creators, there was a large demand for new work.

Impresarios were generally contracted to produce at least one new work in the season, often more. For eager composers there was plenty of work about. However, even a 'new' work might not be as novel as it pretended. Librettos tended to be based on familiar sources; the same libretto, especially those by Metastasio, would be set again and again; and composers indulged in a great deal of recycling of their own (and sometimes other people's) work. In the days before recording, it was astonishing how much an agile composer like Rossini could get away with. But, after all, these people were not trying to produce a masterpiece. Just as the average librettist was a literary hack intent on producing a workable libretto in a short time, the composer too was working to rule, catering to the various restrictions of a particular production and these naturally included the variable capacity of the singers.

Success

After a delay imposed by the illness of two of the singers, Rossini's opera *Tancredi* opened at La Fenice in Venice in February 1813, three weeks before his twenty-first birthday. La Fenice being a more substantial theater than San Moisè and *Tancredi* being a two-act opera, Rossini asked for double the fee, 600 lire, but after some bargaining settled for 500.

This was the opera that really established Rossini's reputation, as it was soon being performed all over Italy and beyond. The libretto, not very distinguished, was based on a novel by Voltaire, set in the time of the Crusades. A well-worn subject, and with an overture borrowed from *La pietra del paragone*, it was not an immediate hit, but within a few months, it is said, people were singing the famous aria, 'Di tanti palpiti' in the streets. This is sometimes called 'the rice aria' because Rossini supposedly composed it in the time taken to boil a pot of rice. The speed at which he worked was already irritating certain jealous critics and provoking accusations of self-plagiarism.

The opera was no revolutionary innovation. It has plenty of *bel canto* and more chorus than customary, but still moves along at a reasonable pace. Rossini took it to Ferrara immediately afterwards, where he made some changes, restoring the story's tragic ending. This version, which seems to have since disappeared, was not welcome however, and the phoney happy ending was restored. As a rule, Rossini was intent to please the audience; though he had his moments of defiance he was not one of those composers who stands exclusively on artistic integrity and ignores popular taste.

Within two months, he was back in Venice, this time at a third theater, the San Benedetto, with an *opera buffa*, *L'Italiana in Algeri* (*The Italian Girl in Algiers*), a work which has featured largely in the twentieth-century revival of Rossini. Based on the story of the slave girl Roxelane beloved of the Ottoman sultan Suleiman the Magnificent, it appealed to the current 'oriental' taste. Again, the subject was not new but the opera is an example of how Rossini broadened the categories: it contains a greater variety of emotions than usual in the *opera buffa* tradition. Rossini did not set out to create new forms, nor did he do so, but from the first he blurred the rigid boundaries, seeming by his reuse of material to consider the same music appropriate to the serious or the comic form and thus reinvigorating the somewhat stagnant *opera seria*.

An early stage design for Tancredi, *by Bozzetto del Sanquirico (Lebrecht)*

At the end of the year 1813 Rossini was in Milan. *Tancredi* had recently been performed at La Scala and, by comparison, his new opera was disappointing. *Aureliano in Palmira* contained a role for the castrato, Giovanni Battista Velluti, whom Rossini admired. He admired him less after this experience, for Velluti caused trouble at rehearsals and insisted on embroidering his music with fancy decoration which Rossini deplored.

In spite of its poor reception, Rossini himself liked the work, especially the overture which he was to use again twice – the second time for *Il barbiere di Siviglia*.

The title page of Aureliano in Palmira *(Lebrecht)*

However, he was temporarily out of luck at La Scala, for the Milanese did not like *Il Turco in Italia*, produced in August 1814, any more than *Aureliano* – less if anything. The trouble stemmed chiefly from the obvious parallel with *L'Italiana in Algeri*. Audiences assumed that the Turk was simply the Italian girl worked over, but this was almost pure imagination. The music was quite different. It was merely the association of the titles that made people assume that Rossini was repeating himself. It is again necessary to remind oneself of the different conditions introduced by the invention of recording. People were not able to make a direct comparison as they could today by listening to the two works on the same day.

Il Turco was not sung again in Milan for seven years. When it was, it proved a great success. At the time, however, it must have seemed that Rossini's genius had been overestimated. Only *Tancredi* and *L'Italiana* maintained his reputation, and his next opera, *Sigismondo* (1814), was a thorough flop. It has remained so, no production being known since his own time in Italy or anywhere else. The basic trouble was a very poor libretto, something that under the system then prevailing the composer could do little or nothing about. The audience at La Fenice, however, were rather kind, according to Rossini. They were obviously bored, he recalled years later, but restrained themselves from expressing their feelings and allowed the work to proceed in silence. To some of his friends, who applauded politely, Rossini remarked that they ought to be whistling.

Somewhat chastened, Rossini returned to Bologna. His activities there included giving music lessons to a niece of Napoleon. The young lady's distinguished uncle was about to stage his final act, causing some trouble to Rossini, not to mention the rest of Europe, in the process.

Joachim Murat, Napoleon's brother-in-law and King of Naples (AKG)

Napoleon escaped from Elba in March 1815. His brother-in-law, Joachim Murat, who was the *de facto* King of Naples, allied himself with Italian nationalism and attempted, without much success, to challenge the Austrians. On April 5 he proclaimed Italian independence, a somewhat empty gesture but enough to set off an enthusiastic rising in Bologna.

In the heady atmosphere, Rossini composed a patriotic 'Inno dell'indipendenza' or 'Hymn of Independence', sung at the Teatro Contavalli in Bologna on April 15, and conducted by Rossini in the presence of Murat. Promptly hailed as 'the Italian *Marseillaise*', it proved to be a lot less popular. Less than twenty-four hours later, the Austrians marched back into Bologna, and the 'Inno dell'indipendenza' was never heard again.

According to a story that went around some time afterwards, Rossini applied the music to different verses, complimentary to Austria, wrapped up the manuscript in ribbons of yellow and black (the Habsburg colors) and presented it to the Austrian commander as a welcome-back present. The composer angrily denied this story, insisting that 'it would have been a cowardice of which Rossini is incapable'. There was nothing at all heroic about Rossini, but he was probably right in maintaining that this improbable story had been made up as a malicious joke.

The truth of Rossini's denial is supported by the activities of the Austrian authorities, who, apprised of the celebration that had so shortly preceded their arrival, marked him down as a dangerous subversive and kept him under surveillance for several years. A less likely revolutionary would be hard to imagine.

In these years Rossini's whereabouts at a given time can best be ascertained from reports of operatic 'first nights' in various cities. Otherwise, information about him is sparse. Rossini's life falls into two parts, and it is unfortunate that the first half, when his genius was fizzing, is far less well documented than the second half, when he composed no operas and very little else.

From Rossini's frequent movements around Italy, it is obvious that he spent a great deal of time traveling. In the pre-railway age this was not a relaxing occupation. Most roads were poor, and travel was both slow – two overnight stops necessary between Rome and Naples – and uncomfortable. Many things could go wrong. The traces might snap and the horses bolt, a wheel might break and the coach overturn, the horses might be sick, the coachman drunk, the coach overloaded, the road flooded... A reported attack on a coach by a lion, presumably escaped from a menagerie, was admittedly an uncommon cause of disaster, but there was no end to the possible predicaments facing travelers. They were well advised to go by boat when that was possible.

These mishaps were common to road travel almost anywhere, but an added menace, in southern Italy especially, was the infestation of the countryside by bandits. At times, certain roads became no-go areas, totally controlled by murderous gangs. Numerous travelers at this period complained of being robbed, some within a few miles of Rome, and the city itself sometimes came under virtual siege, with no one able to leave because of the bandits on the road. However, the danger of robbery – and worse – did not discourage the growing numbers of tourists then any more than it does now. Nor, on the other hand, did the grisly display of the corpses, or parts thereof, of executed bandits along the road do much to discourage their successors (robbery with violence being preferable to death by starvation), though it certainly added to the nervous traveler's anxieties. Sometimes the roads were protected by soldiers, but all travelers went well armed and, if possible, accompanied by armed guards.

The infelicities of travel must have weighed more heavily with Rossini from 1815, when he paid his first visit to Naples. That kingdom, shortly to become 'The Kingdom of the Two Sicilies', had recently been restored to its Bourbon ruler by the Austrians. In fact, Rossini reached the city at about the same time as Prince Leopold, representing his elder brother, King Ferdinand IV. The King himself appeared a month later, to great but misleading acclaim.

The man who brought Rossini to Naples was described by Rossini's biographer, Herbert Weinstock, as 'one of the most interesting figures in early nineteenth-century Italian theatrical life'. He was Domenico Barbaia, born in humble circumstances in Milan in 1778, who

Impresario Domenico Barbaia was responsible for bringing Rossini to Naples (Lebrecht)

began his working life as a waiter. He is alleged to have invented the beverage now called *granita di café*, but he made his fortune by operating the gambling tables at La Scala. He was a born impresario, energetic, intelligent, clever – even crafty – with an unerring eye for a promising opportunity or a talented individual. In 1809 he moved to Naples as a sort of national impresario, controlling the chief opera houses and, equally if not more important, obtaining a license to operate the gambling saloons. He remained in charge there for over thirty years, though also active in enterprises elsewhere, as far away as Vienna.

Barbaia played a part in the careers of several of the chief operatic composers of the early nineteenth century, especially Rossini. The contract they agreed appointed Rossini musical director of the San Carlo and the Fondo theaters and required him to provide two new operas per year. One might suppose that this was a full-time job, but Rossini made sure the contract stipulated that he was free to work elsewhere as and when opportunity arose. Some vigorous haggling took place over the terms of the contract – Rossini satirically remarked that Barbaia would have had him running the kitchens if he could – but the great advantage was that Rossini would now receive a substantial, regular salary, the benefits of which any self-employed artist would confirm.

At first Rossini had to confront a certain amount of prejudice. His arrival in Naples, which still considered itself the operatic center of the world (though the rest of the world was no longer so certain of Naples' preeminence), was announced in the local press without enthusiasm and in a way which suggested, rightly or wrongly, that Neapolitans might never have heard of this 'Signor Rossini', named last in a list of not especially distinguished visitors. He was said to have come 'from Italy'

(Neapolitans did not then consider themselves Italians), which implied a certain threat. Rossini was seen as representing new and alien influences which were out of sympathy with the traditional Neapolitan style. He had been condemned as a degenerate influence by the composer Giovanni Paisiello, an old man (he was to die the following year), but a favorite in Naples in spite of losing some favor as a result of Napoleon's patronage. The director of the Royal College of Music, Zingarelli, was said to have told his students they should not even look at the scores of Rossini's operas for fear of being corrupted.

In other words, Rossini was the wave of the future, and to that extent conservatives were quite right to see him as a threat. The so-called 'Neapolitan school', never a very meaningful term since people like Paisiello were equally active outside Naples, was already fading away.

The subject of Rossini's first opera for the Teatro San Carlo, the largest opera house in Europe, was announced even before the maestro's arrival in the city. Reflecting the popularity of English themes, it was *Elisabetta, regina d'Inghilterra* (*Elizabeth, Queen of England*). The libretto, based on an obscure English novel of 1785, was concerned with the supposed love affair between Elizabeth and Robert Dudley, Earl of Leicester. Any relation to historical facts is largely coincidental, though that did not bother the English tourists in Naples, whose numbers were again increasing after the defeat of Napoleon.

The most important aspect of the opera, and no doubt the most important in Rossini's mind too, was that it gave a cracking role to Isabella Colbran.

The great Spanish soprano was now thirty and her voice was at its peak, though it was soon to show signs of decline. Barbaia had brought her to Naples and, in the

The lush interior of the Teatro di San Carlo, Naples (AKG)

customary manner, she had become his mistress. Very shortly – it is not certain exactly when – she was to transfer her favors to Rossini, and eventually she became his wife, though none of this seems to have affected the amiable relationships of the three parties involved.

For a period, between about 1817 and 1822, Colbran was to have a powerful influence on Rossini's work. In that period, he wrote only one *opera buffa*, although that was surely his true forte (no less an authority than Beethoven told him he should never write anything else). But Colbran was a dramatic singer, at her best in tragedy and not at all suited to comedy. It may seem a pity that, for such a substantial part of his relatively short career as a composer of opera, Rossini was diverted from what most would agree was his greatest strength, but no one can say that if he had composed exclusively *opera buffa* in those years, they would have been better than the operas he wrote for Colbran, which being seldom performed are hard to judge, though critics steeped in the music regard them as underrated.

Elisabetta, regina d'Inghilterra contained some small but significant innovations, or, more accurately, extensions of existing trends. It is the first of Rossini's operas which entirely abjures *recitavo secco* ('dry recitative', i.e. with only keyboard accompaniment). The orchestration in general is unusually rich, probably inspired by the San Carlo orchestra, which was superior to any that Rossini had worked with before. This is also the first opera in which Rossini put his foot down firmly against vocal decoration extemporized by the singers. He knew his singers' voices as well as they did themselves, perhaps better, and was perfectly capable of providing the expected *fioritura* himself. Today's sopranos may find Rossini's vocal line florid, when he was writing for Colbran's special abilities, and the comparatively rare

A romantic view of Rome in 1824. The reality was considerably less picturesque (AKG)

performance of *Elisabetta*, even in Rossini's time, was no doubt due to a lack of singers with Colbran's particular gifts. However, Rossini himself, when a revival was mooted at Florence in 1838, politely declined to have anything to do with the project, remarking that some operas are best 'left at rest'.

The first performance of *Elisabetta* opened the 1815 autumn season at the San Carlo and was attended by the King and the entire court. It was a smash hit, and banished almost at a stroke the prejudice against Rossini as a degenerate northerner. Legend declares that the King afterwards ordered Zingarelli to rescind his ban on Rossini's music. The fact that the universally popular *L'Italiana in Algeri* was playing simultaneously at another theater in the town helped to make Rossini the toast of Naples.

Rossini did not remain long in Naples to enjoy his new popularity. He left the city almost immediately for Rome, where he had undertaken to supervise a production of one of his works at the Teatro Valle. Rossini's more successful operas had been greeted with warm approval in Rome, but he had never had quite the personal triumph there of the kind he had enjoyed in Venice, and now Naples.

Although some urban improvements had been effected in the Napoleonic era, Rome was still a decayed and scruffy city, apparently unable to compete with its own glorious past. The archaeologists had not yet started to arrive in large numbers and, as malaria was still endemic, visitors wisely avoided the city in the summer months. In winter, though, tourism was increasing rapidly. As usual, the English were especially numerous and, according to Byron, especially stupid ('A parcel of staring boobies').

For the Teatro Valle Rossini produced a new opera, *Torvaldo e Dorliska*, an *opera seria* that contained one comic character (more blurring of the boundaries). It was a total fiasco. A writer in the Rome *Notizie del giorno* blamed the 'very dismal and uninteresting libretto which has not awoken Homer from his sleep'. Rossini could afford the occasional flop, in fact he could afford several, as there was now enough of his music being performed to present a wider view of his output. In any case, a week or so before the first performance of *Torvaldo e Dorliska*, he signed a contract for a new *opera buffa* with Duke Sforza-Cesarini, owner and manager of the Teatro di Torre Argentina, which was to lift him indisputably into the ranks of the immortals.

The Barber of Seville

The contract, which still exists, that Rossini agreed to after the usual haggles with Duke Francesco Sforza-Cesarini on December 15, 1815 called for delivery of the completed opera just five weeks later. Moreover, until December 26 Rossini must have been fully occupied with rehearsals for *Torvaldo e Dorliska*, which opened the Carnival season. The time that Rossini actually worked on his most famous opera has been variously estimated, but it would seem that the whole process, from planning to performance, was completed within a maximum of twenty-four days. It was by no means a record for Rossini, who was a notoriously fast worker and used to drive his employers to distraction by his leisurely approach, enjoying the social life of the town before getting down to work at the last moment. Donizetti was even quicker, and the story goes that when he was told how long Rossini had taken to compose *Il barbiere di Siviglia*, he replied, tongue presumably in cheek, that Rossini always worked slowly.

Hostile critics would say that Rossini's speedy productivity was due to the amount of second-hand music he included, and it is true that, like other composers, he made frequent use of earlier work. It was only sensible to retrieve the good bits from an opera that had flopped and seemed never likely to be revived, though Rossini's self-borrowings were not confined to such rescue work. The *Barber* contains several items from *Elisabetta regina d'Inghilterra* and from other, earlier operas, but they are comparatively minor. The critics exaggerated this tendency, sometimes pointing to similarities with works that, had they checked first, they would have realized were written later.

The aria that Rosina sings during the singing lesson became customarily 'Di tanti palpiti' from *Tancredi* (in fact, at the first performance it was something else, chosen by the singer), but since it is a singing lesson this is perfectly reasonable.

Something similar happened with the overture. This is basically the same as the overture written originally for *Aureliano in Palmira*, which was adapted for *Elisabetta*; however, Rossini wrote another overture for the original production.

Besides the draconian deadline, the contract also called for Rossini to accept whatever libretto he was given, to adapt the music according to the individual talents of the singers, to attend all necessary rehearsals and to direct the first three performances from the keyboard. This was all standard procedure, demanding though it seems. The composer's compensation was a fee considerably less than that received by the principal singers – only about one-third of the fee of the renowned tenor, Manuel Garcia, who sang the Count. Sforza-Cesarini did undertake to provide board and lodging, but it is easy to sympathize with the lament of Donizetti that 'the profession of the poor composer of operas is of the unhappiest'.

The Duke was on a tight budget. The Argentina, which was built on his land and owned as well as managed by him, had not been a great financial success and, apart from the necessary big star (Garcia), he was trying to keep production costs as low as possible. He was rather worried that he could not afford dancers, a predilection of Roman audiences.

When the contract was signed, not only did the libretto not exist, the subject was still undecided. Jacopo Ferretti, later to cooperate successfully with Rossini, turned in a libretto which was regarded as unsuitable – too dull. In some desperation,

Sforza-Cesarini turned to Cesare Sterbini, who had written the libretto for *Torvaldo e Dorliska*, regarded in some quarters as largely to blame for that opera's failure. He was reluctant, and only agreed on January 17, promising to deliver the first of the two acts exactly one week later.

As contemporary commentators nearly all remarked, the librettist in Italian opera was a poor hack, often 'some parasitical abbé' according to Stendhal. There were one or two good ones, usually people who had some other, more practical means of support, but by and large, even if their talent was more than mediocre, they had little inducement to do more than go through the motions. This is strange, as many knowledgeable people realized that the libretto is vital to the success of an opera. *The Barber* is in fact a very good example of this.

The subject, possibly suggested by Rossini, was taken from *Le Barbier de Séville* (1775), by Beaumarchais, a most fortuitous choice. Beaumarchais himself had conceived of his play as a kind of musical, and had once staged it as such. It was peculiarly well adapted for comic opera and its obvious affinity with the *commedia dell'arte* tradition made it especially suitable in Italy.

Mozart had of course taken another play by Beaumarchais, with the same characters, for his *Marriage of Figaro*, a promising portent. A more awkward precedent was that *Le Barbier de Séville* had also been appropriated previously for the operatic stage – several times in fact. There was nothing unusual in this. Italian audiences preferred familiar stories, which saved them the bother of having to follow the plot, but in this case embarrassment arose from the fact that *Il barbiere di Siviglia* which everyone knew and remembered had been written by the revered Giovanni Paisiello. There was little doubt that a new version would be taken by Paisiello's

Rossini's autograph of Figaro's Cavatina, Il barbiere di Siviglia *(Lebrecht)*

admirers as presumptuous if not downright offensive.

Considerable efforts were made to avoid trouble. Rossini, describing the gestation of the *Barber* many years later, said that he wrote to Paisiello himself, in flattering terms, and that he received a friendly reply, wishing him good luck with his own version. This was denied by Geltrude Righetti-Giorgi, Rossini's original Rosina whose memoirs are a prime source for this period, but it seems unlikely that Rossini would have lied about it. The printed libretto, handed out according to custom to the audience before the performance, contained an 'advertisement' or preface which attempted to forestall the rage of the *paisiellisti*. It pointed out that Rossini had no desire to 'incur the ill repute of a foolhardy rivalry with the immortal composer who has preceded him', and that this was an entirely different version, different due to passage of time, changing taste, different theaters, etc. To further emphasize the difference, the opera was given a different title,

Almaviva, ossia l'inutile precauzione, (*Almaviva, or the Futile Precaution*), although everyone seems to have called it *Il Barbiere di Siviglia* from the first.

In any case, Rossini's precautions proved insufficient.

The disasters of the first night of *Il barbiere di Siviglia* were not all due to the *paisiellisti*. Under the papal government, opera houses in Rome were, strictly speaking, illegal. There were generally ways around such repressive laws, and the opera houses survived by adopting the category of temporary buildings. That meant they were built of wood, and thus even more vulnerable to the threat of fire, which afflicted more substantial buildings like the San Carlo in Naples which had burned down a week before the *Barber* opened. They also tended to be shabby, and the general standard of production was very low. The musicians were much poorer than those in Naples, for example. Rossini was surprised when the barber who came to shave him in the morning left with the words, 'See you later.' It transpired he was also a clarinettist in the Argentina orchestra. Indeed, all the members of the orchestra had other jobs.

Descriptions of Roman opera productions by critical visitors, such as the brilliant German musician Ludwig Spohr who was in Rome at about this time, would suggest comic exaggeration were they not so numerous. According to Spohr, it was quite common, while some dramatic aria was being sung, for the rest of the cast to be chatting and joking in the wings. Things had not improved much by the time Berlioz and Mendelssohn recorded their impressions. According to Mendelssohn, the violinists, who were few in number, would play their own variations at will, so that the impression they made was 'more like the din an orchestra makes when it is warming up and tuning'.

Costume designs for the principal characters in Il barbiere di Siviglia, *1830 (AKG)*

The fiasco of the first night of the *Barber* might have been foreseen. Apart from the simmering hostility of a large section of the audience, the impresario Sforza-Cesarini, though only forty-four, died suddenly less than two weeks before the opening. The dismal conditions of the theater were blamed even for this: the Duke had been complaining of the extreme cold of the theater not long before he caught a chill that led to pneumonia and death. Since a lot of money was tied up in the production, the Duke's executors took over and the production went ahead.

On opening night, February 20, the audience, or a large section of it, was more or less looking for trouble. Rossini, not yet twenty-four years old, took his place at the keyboard wearing a jacket described as in the Spanish style, with gold buttons, which had been given to him by Barbaia. This attracted unfriendly jeers. Worse was to come. Zenobio Vitarelli, playing Basilio, fell over a trap as he made his entrance and had to sing his aria with a heavy nose bleed, stanching the blood with a handkerchief as often as he took breath. The audience thought this was tremendous fun, demanded an encore, and altogether made 'an abominable hubbub'. Next, a cat invaded the stage, was chased off by Luigi Zamboni (Figaro), but promptly appeared from the other side, leaping into the arms of a shocked Bartolommeo Botticelli (Bartolo) and, having been expelled from that haven, raced about all over the stage, scattering the other performers. This was even better! The cat received a crescendo of encouragement from the delighted audience, loud meows mixing with catcalls of other varieties.

When Righetti-Giorgi made her first entrance as Rosina, she was piercingly whistled. Her duet with Figaro was almost drowned out. Rossini himself, subjected to 'indescribable' abuse, displayed more moral stamina than he is usually credited

*The brilliant
German
musician,
Ludwig Spohr
(Mansell)*

A sculpture caricature of Lablache as Figaro, mocking the singer's size (Lebrecht/Private Collection)

with. At the end of the first act, with moderate turmoil prevailing in the auditorium, he stood and calmly applauded the singers. Some of the audience thought, or pretended to think, that he was applauding his own work, which further incensed them.

What was Rossini's reaction to this disaster? Unfortunately, it is difficult to say, not because no one described it but because individual descriptions contradict each other. According to Righetti-Giorgi he left the theater early with an appearance of complete indifference. Later she went to his house to comfort him, but found her sympathy was unnecessary: he was sleeping peacefully.

The next night, having made some changes in the score, he stayed at home feigning illness. The second performance was listened to in an orderly manner and greeted with prolonged applause. When the singers went to Rossini's house afterwards, they found him surrounded by distinguished citizens of Rome who had come to congratulate him on his great success!

Another account describes Rossini under siege on this second night, awoken from sleep by a commotion outside and, fearful that the crowd was going to set fire to the house, taking refuge in a stable at the back. There Garcia found him and assured him that the crowd had come to acclaim, not to lynch him. He would have none of it: 'To hell with them and their bravos!' Garcia returned to attempt some expiatory speech, but someone threw an orange at him and he had a black eye for a week.

Il barbiere di Siviglia has long been universally acclaimed as Rossini's greatest work. A couple of generations ago, it was the only Rossini opera that most people knew, and the only one performed, though it has always been performed frequently. That situation has changed, Rossini is more popular than at any time since his own, but the opera *Il barbiere di Siviglia* is still his most popular work.

It is not that it contains Rossini's best music – at least, it is rivaled in that respect by many other operas. As usual in Rossini, it is not so much the melody of the vocal line as the orchestration that achieves the finest effects, but what chiefly distinguishes the *Barber* is the excellence of the libretto. Not only was Beaumarchais' play particularly suitable, Sterbini's libretto made the most of the splendid opportunities it offered. It has far more drive and energy than the libretto for Paisiello's version – which, of course, Sterbini was no doubt able to consult, both for points to follow and points to avoid. It is also simpler. The deeper social and political connotations present in Beaumarchais and in Paisiello have disappeared. Figaro, for instance, is a different character. In Rossini he is a straightforward comedy figure, and – to some extent reflecting Italian society – there is no trace of class warfare in the relations between count and barber. Something is undoubtedly lost, but perhaps well lost, for there is a gain in sheer dynamism. Clarity of motivation energizes character and plot.

Finally, the whole work is infected with those champagne qualities for which Rossini is famous – his sheer zest and high spirits, his speed, grace, elegance, and wit, his brisk avoidance of sentimentality.

Verdi summed up the matter in 1898 in a letter of thanks to an author who had sent him a copy of his book about musicians: 'You say many things about Rossini and Bellini, and they may be true, but I confess that I cannot help believing *Il barbiere di Siviglia*, for abundance of ideas, for comic verve, and for truth of declamation, the most beautiful opera buffa in existence.'

*Guiseppe Verdi, composer, a
great admirer of Rossini's*
Il barbiere di Siviglia
(Mansell)

Celere

After the *Barber*, Rossini hastened back to Naples which, if someone leading so peripatetic an existence can be said to have a home town, was for a few years Rossini's. He found the San Carlo a blackened ruin, and the company occupying the Teatro del Fondo, where Rossini's cantata for a wedding in the royal family, a rather long and elaborate piece called 'Le Nozze di Teti e di Peleo', was performed at the end of April. (The score disappeared but was rediscovered some years ago in Naples by the Rossini scholar Philip Gossett.)

Rossini's second Naples opera was an *opera buffa* called *La gazzetta*, the libretto based on a play by the Venetian playwright Carlo Goldoni. Despite one very good comic role and a couple of appealing arias, it was not a success, and was never performed again in the composer's lifetime.

Very different was its successor, a three-act *opera seria*, *Otello*, first produced in December 1816. Ultimately, Rossini's *Otello* was to suffer the same fate he had brought upon Paisiello with *Il barbiere*: it was swept from the repertoire by Verdi's masterpiece of 1887. Until then, however, it was performed quite regularly, the second act often on its own.

Not many Italians in 1816 knew much about Shakespeare, few of whose plays had even been translated, and this was just as well, for the libretto played fast and loose with the Swan of Avon. It was written by the Marchese Francisco Berio di Salsa, a cultured man with a wide knowledge of literature, a fine host and conversationalist, but without much creative ability. The opera centers, more than the play, on

Karl Friedrich Schinkel's stage design for Act I of Otello *(AKG)*

Rossini wears the uniform of the French Academy.
The score of Otello *lies open on his right*
(Lebrecht)

Desdemona, because that role was destined for Colbran. Curiously, the two other great sopranos of the time who sang Desdemona, Maria Malibran (daughter of Manuel Garcia) and Giuditta Pasta, were dissatisfied with the part and preferred to essay the role of Otello – something not too unusual then, odd as it seems now.

The making of the opera, as Meyerbeer pointed out when he saw it in Venice in 1818, is the remarkable third act, which for tragic intensity measures up to Verdi. Meyerbeer called it

> *god-like, and what is so extraordinary… absolutely anti-Rossini-ish. First-rate declamation, ever-impassioned recitative, mysterious accompaniment full of local colour, and, particularly, the style of the oldtime romances at its highest perfection.*

Rossini was professionally more at home in Naples than in Rome. Some critics find him more expansive in his Naples operas, and no doubt he felt liberated by the generally higher standard of production and musicianship. But, as it happens, his two most popular comic operas were both written for Rome.

Before leaving Rome after the *Barber*, he had contracted to write an opera for his friend Pietro Cartoni at the Teatro Valle, and as soon as *Otello* was launched, he obtained all the necessary passes to get out of Naples, prepared himself for the innumerable customs halts along the way, and headed for Rome again.

As usual, the deadline for the new opera loomed with no subject decided and therefore no libretto. When one was at last produced, it fell foul of the censors, so Jacopo Ferretti was summoned at short notice. He left an account of what followed.

It was December 23. The original opening date had been December 26, but not even Rossini could write an opera with no libretto in two days, so it was put off until January 25. Ferretti, Cartoni and Rossini gathered in Cartoni's apartment, shivering from the cold and drinking tea. Ferretti suggested one idea after another, twenty or thirty he reckoned, but there was always some objection. The hour grew late. Rossini took to the bed, ostensibly so he could think better. Ferretti, half asleep himself, murmured something about 'Cinderella', and Rossini shot up in bed. How soon could he have the outline? Ferretti, inspired by this unexpectedly positive reaction, said he would work all night and give it to Rossini in the morning.

He was as good as his word. Subsequently he wrote the libretto, so he said, in twenty-two days. Rossini wrote the music in twenty-four.

Not surprisingly, the first night of *La Cenerentola* was chaotic, though not quite as bad as the *Barber*. Rossini, who always had an unerring idea of his own worth, was

Maria Malibran, opera singer
and friend of Rossini
(Lebrecht/Private Collection)

A scene from the first performance of La Gazza Ladra, *1817 (Lebrecht)*

not disconcerted by its poor reception. He knew it was good, and posterity proved him right. *La Cenerentola* is today probably his most popular opera after the Barber.

Good or bad, he could not hang around. After a brief stop in Bologna, presumably visiting his parents and commiserating with them on the recent death of his grandmother, who had been partly responsible for his upbringing, he traveled to Milan to fulfill a contract with La Scala. The result of this was *La gazza ladra* (*The Thieving Magpie*). In spite of the pastoral setting, it was really an *opera seria*, though Rossini was not greatly restricted by these distinctions and liked to exploit the more liberal conventions of the *opera buffa*. The relatively complex orchestration of *La gazza ladra* was ascribed, perhaps correctly, to German influence.

It was a great success and must have sent Rossini off to Naples again, in August 1817, in good spirits. The new San Carlo was finished, though the plaster was still wet and the candle lighting made the walls steam alarmingly. It was even larger – too large for all but the biggest voices – and more magnificent than before. The royal box was supported by gilded palm trees. Rossini's first offering in these ornate surroundings, *Armida*, in November 1817, was not very well received, and this time he was unable to repeat his recent successes in Rome the following month, where *Adelaida di Borgogna* aroused no enthusiasm; nor has it since.

Back in Naples, he was compelled to set a biblical subject, as it would be produced during Lent. *Moisè in Egitto* (*Moses in Egypt*) opened in March 1818. It was an ambitious work, and the production was complicated by the current political hostility between monarchists and liberals. Colbran, admired by the King, was the symbol of the monarchists, and Rossini was inevitably associated with that party. The Liberals went so far as to sponsor a rival opera, though the troubles of *Moisè in*

Egitto were due more to the usual production difficulties than to competition.

In the original production, the parting of the Red Sea defied the ingenuity of the designers, and caused more laughter than awe. On the whole, however, the opera could be counted a success, and the Liberals were confounded. In the revised production next year Rossini added the prayer, 'Dal tuo stellato soglio', to cover the stage mechanics involved in the parting of the Red Sea. This became the most notable piece in the whole opera, which is also interesting for giving the main role to a bass instead of the usual tenor. Good tenors, then as now, were fairly thick on the ground in Italy. Basses, with fewer opportunites, were more rare.

In the summer of 1818 Rossini was back in his home town, Pesaro. The theater there had been newly restored, and the town's most distinguished citizen consented to open it with a production of *La gazza ladra*. He was the producer as well as director, hiring the singers and orchestral players, and he took a great deal of trouble over it. Rossini was eventually to fall out of fashion largely because he was seen as a not sufficiently serious musician. His own easy-going, sardonic approach to life encouraged this erroneous impression. But Rossini saw himself as a professional, not as a fabulous creative genius. It is an attitude, some might say, greatly to be commended. It did not prevent him bringing to the music of the nineteenth century what Francis Toye called a whiff of an exciting perfume, not to mention a hearty laugh, which are more than welcome in the twentieth century.

In Pesaro Rossini suffered an illness severe enough to give rise to reports in some places that he had died. On the contrary, he was soon back to his usual frenetic activity. In August he was in Bologna, where he was commissioned to write a one-act work for Lisbon, *Adina*. For some reason it was not performed there until several years later. In December *Riccardio e Zoraide* opened at the San Carlo, with libretto again by Berio. It was warmly greeted at the time but later sank into oblivion. Rossini was busy writing a cantata to celebrate the King's recovery from illness – the orchestra included 120 wind instruments – and with mounting a new Lenten production of *Moisè in Egitto*. He was also working on two new operas, *Ermione*, also doomed to obscurity, and *Edoardo e Cristina*, for Venice. The latter, performed by top singers and received ecstatically, was nothing but a pastiche: it contained only seven newly composed pieces out of a total of twenty-six, the remainder being garnered from works the Venetians had not heard yet. This is the sort of thing that got Rossini a bad name. On the other hand, impresarios were satisfied with what they paid for, and Rossini could not have maintained such a rate of productivity without resorting to scissors and paste on some scale.

On his way back to Naples, Rossini again paused at Pesaro, for what seems to have been the last time. He had made himself unpopular with a small but rowdy section of the populace. They were adherents of the unlovable Princess Caroline of Brunswick, alienated wife of the English Prince Regent, who was at that period living outside Pesaro with her Italian lover. On his previous visit Rossini, following the example of his hosts, had declined to call on the Princess, and now, on visiting the theater, he was harassed by a crowd and had to leave by a side entrance.

In Naples a week later, at the beginning of June, Rossini had a conversation with a young French musician who told him that he had just been reading a poem which, he thought, would make a fine subject for an opera. The poem turned out to be a translation of Sir Walter Scott's *The Lady of the Lake*. Rossini borrowed the book and, liking it, handed it over to one of Barbaia's librettists. *La donna del lago* opened at

Singer Giuseppina Ronzi de Begnis wears a typically lavish 'oriental' costume in an 1822 version of Mosè in Egitto *(Lebrecht/Private Collection)* the San Carlo on September 24, 1819, Colbran making her first appearance in a boat on a lake.

Though it was soon to become one of his most popular operas, the Neapolitans did not take to it at first. According to one story, vehemently denied by Rossini, their unresponsive reception caused him to faint. The lack of enthusiasm probably stemmed from surprise, for this was not exactly what people had come to expect from Rossini. Whether or not the Scottish setting was responsible, this was almost a full-blown Romantic opera, with 'unwonted luxuriance of orchestral and choral sound … now lyric, now epic, now dramatic'.

People soon began to come around, but Rossini could not wait: before the end of October he was off to Milan and his next opera for La Scala. This was another quickie, *Bianca e Falliero*. It was almost bereft of new ideas and incorporated much that was familiar to the Milanese, as well as – another device to spin things out which Rossini occasionally resorted to – long stretches of recitavo secco.

At the end of the busy year of 1819, Rossini, though only twenty-seven, could look back upon what could be regarded as a lifetime's work. Besides cantatas, songs and various pieces of instrumental music, he had written thirty operas, all but one of them in the preceding nine years. Recently, besides fine works, he had produced some dross. He may have felt that, for his health or his reputation, or both, it was time to slow down. At any rate, during the next four years he was to write only four operas and, although only one, perhaps two, would find much favor with posterity, all were carefully composed and largely original.

Whether his reduced output meant that he worked less hard is not easy to say. He was, after all, not merely a composer, but a director of opera, and we catch glimpses of him in Naples working hard on new productions of other composers' work besides his own. He was busy enough to enlist some help with a mass he composed at short notice in March, which someone described as 'a ragout of phrases from Rossinian opera', and he was still under contract to supply new operas to Naples.

To this obligation he returned in the spring, with *Maometto II*, better known in the revised form that Rossini presented in Paris six years later as *Le Siège de Corinthe* Although completed in May or thereabouts, it was not actually performed at the San Carlo until December. The delay was no doubt caused by political events in Naples that year: a liberal revolution resulted in the temporary flight of the King, not for the first time, and the arrival of Austrian troops to restore the status quo in March 1821. There were few casualties throughout the affair, which had a pronounced air of comic opera itself: a debate in the new revolutionary parliament on whether God was the author of Universal Law was decided, so the British ambassador reported, 'in favour of the Deity by a small majority'.

Having spent most of the year 1820 in Naples, Rossini returned to Rome in December. There he renewed his acquaintance with the famous violin virtuoso, Paganini, who had given a series of concerts in Naples the previous year. They indulged in some high jinks during the carnival masquerade, dressing up as blind female street entertainers. Paganini also stepped into the breach to conduct the first performance of Rossini's *Matilde Shabran* after the musical director of the Teatro Apollo died of a heart attack the day before.

That sad misfortune was but one aggravation in the customary scramble to get a Rossini opera underway. The original libretto had been slow to arrive and uninteresting when it did, so once again Ferretti was called to the rescue. But, according to one story, Rossini was unable to complete the score without help, and summoned assistance in the form of Giovanni Pacini, another highly productive composer who was eventually to write nearly one hundred operas, mostly in a Rossinian style. 'I am still short six pieces', Rossini is alleged to have told Pacini. 'You compose three and I'll compose three. Here is paper and a chair – write!'

The opera was not well received, and the impresario who had hired Rossini refused to pay the last part of his fee. Rossini hurried to the theater and gathered up the score and all the musicians' parts. The impresario was left with the choice of paying up or canceling further performances. As the opera continued to be performed until the end of the season, he presumably paid up.

Rossini returned to Naples, but his thoughts were now venturing farther afield. He had received an invitation to compose an opera for the King's Theatre in London. Vienna also beckoned, and so did Paris where, despite notoriously poor standards of production, Rossini's operas were hugely popular. The genial Barbaia was prepared to renegotiate their agreement, allowing Rossini to take up these invitations with the assumption, never to be fulfilled, that he would in due course return to Naples.

Rossini's last Naples opera, *Zelmira*, was really composed for Vienna, but was given a trial run at the San Carlo in February 1822. Though Naples was usually kind, and there was much enthusiasm on the first night, the opera did not hold great appeal for the Neapolitans. It was to prove more successful farther north, in Vienna itself for instance, and thus indicated the path that the composer himself would shortly take.

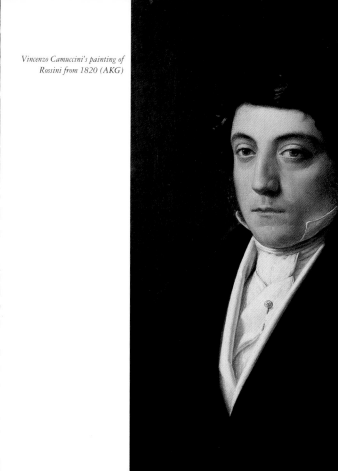

*Vincenzo Camuccini's painting of
Rossini from 1820 (AKG)*

Niccolo Paganini, composer, violinist and conductor (Mansell)

London

In March 1822 Rossini married Isabella Colbran. She had been his mistress for several years – probably since 1817 – and there was not much romance attached to the wedding. Rossini said he did it for his mother's sake, and would just as soon have remained single. There is a suspicion that financial considerations were not absent from his thoughts. Colbran was wealthy, with estates in Sicily as well as her villa at Castenaso, near Bologna, while Rossini, though now earning large fees, had so far never been able to save any money. On the other hand, Colbran was much older, and her voice was in decline. As so often happens, the apparent success of an illicit relationship faded away once it was formalized.

The wedding took place at Castenaso as the couple were on their way to Vienna. Rossini's first venture outside Italy was due to the ubiquitous Barbaia, who had become impresario of Vienna's Kärnthnerthortheater and imported not only Rossini but also a team of Italian singers. This trip marks the beginning of Rossini's conquest of Europe, in its way as victorious as Napoleon's, in the course of which he attracted the kind of adulation nowadays associated with pop stars. Correspondingly, the dignitaries of the musical academies tended to be critical.

In Vienna he faced some stiff competition: Beethoven, Schubert and Weber were all in town, the latter to conduct his *Der Freischütz*, which Rossini heard soon after his arrival. Of these four famous composers it was Rossini who was the main center of attention. It is doubtful if he met Weber, who was extremely hostile to Rossini's music on this occasion, though they established friendly relations later. Rossini did,

Isabella Colbran (AKG)

Composer, Richard Wagner (AKG)

however, have a famous meeting with Ludwig van Beethoven.

Rossini had probably not heard a great deal of Beethoven's music, but in Vienna he heard the *Eroica* symphony. '[It] overwhelmed me,' he remembered many years later, and 'I had only one thought, to meet this great genius ...'

Rossini later gave more than one account of his meeting with Beethoven, much the longest and – suspiciously – most detailed in a conversation with a fascinated Richard Wagner nearly forty years afterwards.

The meeting was hard to arrange, and when achieved, communication was not easy. By this time Beethoven was stone deaf and steeped in misanthropy, seeming older than his fifty-two years. Rossini could not speak German, though Beethoven knew some Italian. The great man was, nevertheless, reasonably encouraging. He had read the score of the *Barber* with enjoyment, and advised Rossini to stick to *opera buffa*. 'Make a lot of Barbers!'

Shocked by the squalor in which Beethoven was living – very different from his own circumstances – Rossini made some attempt to start a collection for him in Vienna, but he was assured that Beethoven lived as he did because he wanted to. There was some truth in this no doubt, though perhaps not enough.

Rossini's operas were well known in Vienna, a city that traditionally prefers its music on the light side, but their performance by an Italian company was something of a revelation. The opening production, *Zelmira*, was handicapped by Colbran's indisposition, but it was carefully prepared by Rossini and conducted by the resident conductor, Joseph Weigl, who was determined to provide no ammunition for those who regarded him as an anti-Rossinian.

The whole season was a spectacular success, in financial as well as musical terms, and Rossini for once did not rush away after the last night.

After one or two other visits, he and his wife retired to Castenaso, where Rossini opened negotiations for the purchase of his own palazzo in Bologna, but the prospect of a quiet autumn, working on a new opera for the Carnival season in Venice, was disrupted by a summons from Prince Metternich, the presiding genius of post-Napoleonic Europe. He invited Rossini to the Congress of Verona (October 1822), the latest of the regular four-power conferences instituted in 1815, which was bedeviled by the British objection to the despatch of French troops to suppress a rebellion in Spain. Metternich, in a happy phrase, invited the 'god of harmony' to come to Verona where harmony was so badly needed.

In bestowing harmony upon the assembled statesmen Rossini was not altogether successful, as Britain soon walked out of the congress in dudgeon, but the social side of the event was much enhanced by two Rossini operas, and two cantatas (both now lost) which he wrote especially for the occasion.

Early in December the Rossinis were in Venice. The contract which Rossini had signed with La Fenice called for him to prepare a new version of *Maometto II* as well as a new opera in which Colbran would have the chief role. This, Rossini's last Italian opera, was *Semiramide*.

In many ways it provided a distinguished conclusion to his Italian career. The origin of the story was Voltaire's *Semiramis* and the libretto was by Gaetano Rossi, also the librettist for *Tancredi*. It was an extremely popular story among operatic librettists, and appears to have been used, altogether, about forty times.

Whether or not Rossini was inspired by the somewhat grotesque plot, he wrote some very good music for it (also some not so good) and completed it in thirty-three days. Today, it is the overture that is most familiar. It is fashioned around themes from the opera itself, uncommon in Rossini, and was described by Francis Toye as 'a splendid composition alike as regards thematic material, form, treatment and scoring', its almost symphonic character suggesting that Rossini's visit to Beethoven was still in his mind. There are also many good things in the opera itself and, in the first-act finale, one of the best examples of Rossini's famous, breath-shortening, prolonged crescendos. Though accounts of its initial reception vary, there seems to be no basis for the legend that Rossini was so disgusted with the Venetian audience that he declared he would write no more operas for Italy.

Semiramide capped Rossini's international stature. He was not only the most popular composer of the day, he was the most popular composer there had ever been. And not only in Italy: he was hugely popular throughout Europe as well as much of South America and Mexico. In the Ottoman Empire, it is said, the Sultan's soldiers paraded to a band playing marches from Rossini operas. He handled all this fame with his usual, slightly sardonic good humor. Though much more sensitive than he liked to appear, Rossini was well able to cope with fame and with money. He was socially adept, and he was a shrewd investor.

His experience in Vienna helped to convince Rossini that he should travel farther, but for most of the year 1823 he was more sedentary than usual, spending the summer and early autumn in the Castenaso villa: his own villa in Bologna was not ready for occupation as extensive improvements were being made. He was contracted to the London impresario, Giovanni Battista Benelli, who had already presented many of his operas to English audiences at the King's Theatre. But before going to London in December, the Rossinis spent a month in Paris.

Rossini in 1823: that year his opera Semiramide *had brought him international stature (Mansell)*

His enthusiastic reception in the French capital, a city to which Italy could offer no rival, probably decided Rossini's future course. He was plunged immediately into the customary social whirl and, wherever he went, he was dogged by eager crowds. Bands serenaded him in his apartment opposite the Bibliothèque Nationale, and a huge banquet was arranged in his honor. It was attended by the stars of the theatrical and musical world, and at least one artist, Horace Vernet, whose current mistress, Olympe Pélissier, was one day to be Rossini's second wife. It was a great occasion. Flattering speeches were made and toasts drunk to all and sundry, Rossini himself briefly proposing 'Mozart!' In fact the affair created such wide interest that it became the subject of a satire written partly by the famous librettist and dramatist Eugène Scribe and called *Rossini à Paris, ou Le Grand Dîner.*

At the numerous other social events which notable visitors were expected to attend, Rossini entertained the guests with arias from his operas, accompanying himself on the piano. A royal official approached him with an offer to work for the Théâtre-Italien, but boggled at the salary Rossini demanded.

There was also, not surprisingly, some hostility, some chauvinistic protests at what one anti-Rossinian called 'this paroxysm of Italian fever'. When Rossini was proposed for associate membership of the Académie des Beaux-Arts, the musicians voted against 'Signor Crescendo', as one of them named him – the nickname stuck – and it was the artists who clinched the result in his favor.

After a rough Channel crossing which prostrated Rossini, already suffering with a cold and always susceptible to sea-sickness, for days, the esteemed couple arrived in London and took up residence in Nash's newly revamped Regent Street, not far from the King's Theatre. Tradition says that Rossini used to view the passing crowd from

The King's Theatre, London where in 1824
eight Rossini operas were staged (Lebrecht)

the top of Nash's colonnade in company with a parrot of spectacular hues.

London, like Paris, was a far bigger, richer and livelier city than Rome or Venice, and Rossini found plenty of people known to him from his years in Naples. As in Paris, he was the lion of the social season and moved constantly from one grand salon to another.

It was not long before he received an invitation from the royal court. He first met George IV, no longer quite the 'First Gentleman of Europe' and even more corpulent than Rossini himself, at Brighton, the Royal Pavilion providing a highly appropriate setting. Rossini was not overawed by him and allegedly treated the King with some familiarity; this was the occasion when he sang Desdemona's aria in falsetto, regarded by some as in poor taste since it suggested imitation of the castrato, repugnant to English feelings. Still, it probably sounded better than the choruses in which the King insisted on joining although, as one courtier remarked, 'his voice is not good, and he does not sing so much from notes as from recollection'.

The upper-class gossip, Captain Gronow, who thought that Rossini 'has more of the Englishman than the Italian in his personal appearance' (a judgment with which it is hard to agree), recorded that the King, 'though a great lover of music, and not a bad player on the violin, constantly put out the maestro, to whom he at last offered an apology. Rossini accepted it with civility, and good-naturedly said, "There are few in Your Majesty's position who could play so well."'

It was possible for a foreign musician to earn a great deal of money in London. Rossini could certainly command large fees, though, oddly enough, Colbran could still command even larger ones. However, even she could not rise to the commercial heights commanded by Angelica Catalani, said to have netted £22,000 from one English tour in 1807. Rossini was pleased to discover that he could charge £50 for a public appearance. It was his personality as much as his music, already immensely popular, which made him such a success in society, and no remotely musical gathering could succeed in his absence. Although he sometimes sang himself at these engagements, more often he acted as accompanist for Colbran. For one evening appearance he was paid in shares, which he was afterwards able to sell for £300.

He could also charge up to £100 a time for singing lessons. These were not to be taken too seriously, and were probably more like a private audience, offering rich and untalented people the opportunity to say they had been taught by the great Rossini. The story that the Duke of Wellington, who had entertained Rossini in Verona, was among his singing pupils can surely be discounted.

The concerts and recitals included appearances outside London, notably in Cambridge, where Rossini played the organ in Great St. Mary's and sang his most famous party piece, 'Largo al Factotum' from the *Barber*, in the Senate House. And of

The opera singer Giuditta Pasta in Tancredi *(Lebrecht)*

course there were operas. During the 1824 season no less than eight Rossini operas were to be heard at the King's Theatre, with Italian singers including Manuel Garcia, Giuditta Pasta and others equally famous ('Rossini's music,' the philosopher Hegel, a fan, once wrote in a letter to his wife, 'is made for Italian throats, just as velvets and silks are made for elegant young women'). Rossini directed all of these productions. Again his fees were high, and his London sojourn finally made him, in his own right, a comparatively rich man. He was a good businessman with a keen eye for his own interests, and could be very tough in their defense.

If Rossini's activities in London seem slightly cynical, that was nothing compared with less famous musicians like the less than competent flute player encountered by Rossini himself who earned a handsome income by giving lessons in singing and the piano. There were other examples of people, like the Christopher Isherwood character in the pre-war Berlin of the thirties, who gave lessons on instruments they could not play themselves. Everyone knew that London was a great place for money, but not for music.

Rossini remarked that when in Italy he did not like to accept money simply for accompanying a singer, but he found that in London it was the custom, 'so I followed it like everyone else'. He was the last person to turn down the chance of making an easy buck and, as he remarked, foreign musicians in London were there only to make money. He recounted an incident early in his stay, when at an evening party he encountered two well-known Italian instrumentalists. He assumed they were present to play solos, but they told him they were merely accompanists like himself. 'Have you got your parts?' he asked them. 'No,' they replied, 'we improvise.'

The sojourn of Rossini in London was altogether more of a social success than a triumph of musical creativity. Apart from a 'Lament for the Death of Lord Byron' (1823), London was offered no new compositions. Although he had contracted to write an entirely new opera for Benelli and the King's Theatre, this work never appeared. Benelli, who had not counted the cost of mounting the Rossini season (he paid out over £1,000 on singers' fees alone), was in serious debt, and this may have caused Rossini to hold back. There was talk of an opera called *La figlia dell'aria* (*The Daughter of the Air*), but this was probably *Semiramide* under another name. It was in the London production of this opera, incidentally, that Pasta made her debut in the title role.

In June, when it was finally admitted that the new opera was not forthcoming, Benelli commissioned another, for the next season, *Ugo re d'Italia*. Rossini was never paid for this either, but he must have written at least some of it because, several years later, he wrote asking that the score, plus the bond for £400 that he had been required to deposit, should be returned to him. Apparently he got the money but not the score, which subsequently disappeared somewhere in the dusty offices of a succession of London solicitors and has never been traced.

A long time before he was due to leave London, Rossini was considering other plans. His success in London, and talk of him being lured there on a more permanent basis, had reactivated the French. The French ambassador in London was instructed to offer him a one-year contract on the same terms as had been discussed in Paris some weeks earlier, requiring him to compose a grand opera for the Académie Royale de Musique (i.e. the Paris Opera), and another for the Théâtre-Italien, but this time the remuneration was fixed at what Rossini had asked for. The contract was signed on February 27, two days before the composer's thirty-second birthday.

The Rossinis left London in July, the month his year's contract with the French Court officially began, and in spite of expectations to the contrary, never returned. According to an anecdote ascribed to Rossini in much later years, he had been put off London when he was briefly arrested for debt. Under the laws then current, this could easily happen to almost anyone, though there seems to be no record of it happening to Rossini who, on the contrary, expressed affection for London and appreciation of the almost unprecedented attention he received there. He was happy and his health was good, a combination too easily taken for granted and one which was to elude him for many of his remaining years.

London, England, painted in 1820 (AKG)

Paris

When Rossini arrived in Paris in August 1824 with a one-year contract, he was asked, in addition to the agreed commitments, to take over the directorship of the Théâtre-Italien. This put him in a somewhat delicate situation, since the Théâtre-Italien already had a director, no less a figure than Ferdinando Paër, himself the composer of some forty operas. Paër belonged to the anti-Rossinian party and had, according to his critics, shown little enthusiasm for staging Rossini's operas. Nevertheless, Rossini did not want to upset him, still less put him out of work. Paër's first reaction was to resign, but he withdrew his resignation when he discovered that it meant he would also lose the concomitant court post of *maître de chapelle*. A compromise was patched up, with the two men as co-directors, though it must have been galling for Paër, reduced to a virtual cipher, and he did resign finally two years later.

A few months before the arrival of Rossini in Paris, Stendhal had published his biography of the composer. As a biography, the book is almost completely useless, but biography was not Stendhal's real purpose. The book was full of very readable though unreliable gossip about the Italian musical scene, but essentially it was a work of propaganda. Stendhal was the most persuasive of the large group of people who saw that French opera was languishing and believed it could best be revived by an injection of Italian dynamism.

In Stendhal's view, the basic problems stemmed from current methods of organization and management. Both the Académie Royale de Musique, i.e. the Paris

*Henri Beyle Stendhal, author
of such classic novels as*
Scarlet and Black *and
biographer of Rossini (AKG)*

Opéra, and the Théâtre-Italien came under a minister of the royal court and, under him, a Director of Fine Arts, who at this time was a rich aristocrat, the Vicomte de la Rochefoucauld. He was a good judge of horses but an ignoramus on the subject of music. He is said to have once remarked to Cherubini – at the time, before his premature retirement, probably the outstanding operatic composer in Paris – that he ought to try his hand at writing an opera!

With such a man in charge, it is hardly surprising that artistic standards were notoriously low, but not all the blame can be placed on Rochefoucauld. The Opéra paid high fees, so that, in spite of inexecrable productions, composers were more than willing to write for it. Unfortunately, good composers were thin on the ground, especially after Cherubini and Spontini had left the scene.

High fees and poor productions ran the enterprise seriously into debt, and there were doubts whether it could survive at all. At the Théâtre-Italien the situation under Paër's direction was not a great deal better, and artistic standards were equally low. Stendhal accused Paër of trying to keep Rossini's works off the stage, but there seems to be no substance in the charge: at least twelve Rossini operas were produced at the Théâtre-Italien during his tenure, and in spite of allegedly inferior productions, they were very popular.

Rossini's most famous opera, the *Barber*, could be heard in Paris in 1824 at another venue, the Théâtre de l'Odéon, where a well-meaning amateur impresario, Castil-Blaze, mounted his own, Frenchified version. He followed it with a similarly rehashed, French version of Weber's *Der Freischütz*, and although the productions hardly offered a fair basis for judgment, anti-Rossinians were quick to make odious comparisons. The *Gazette de France*, always hostile to Rossini after its involvement on the opposite side in a legal dispute over copyright, remarked that 'In M. de Weber's music one would look in vain for that wretched luxury of deafening notes, that chattering of ritornellos, that uniform sequence of suborned crescendos which so uselessly inflate the scores of the Italian Orpheus'. However strongly one may disagree with this criticism, it must be admitted that one knows what the critic is talking about! Nevertheless Rossini appeared to shrug off such notices, his usual *sangfroid* undented.

The answer to the fundamental problems of French opera, in the view of Stendhal and others who shared his opinion, was privatization: to remove the theaters from government control and run them as a commercial business. That was how most theaters were run in Italy. As a further step, he advocated the presence in Paris of Rossini, the greatest operatic composer of the day, who would reinvigorate the opera in Paris as he had done in his native country.

Both Stendhal's recommendations were adopted: Rossini was brought to Paris in 1824, and the Opéra was handed over to an independent impresario – though not until after the revolution of 1830. Other factors – the work of Meyerbeer for example – were also partly responsible for the blossoming of French opera that dates from about this time, but clearly Stendhal's recipe was a good one.

In spite of his carefully cultivated laid-back attitude, Rossini studied the task ahead of him with care and proceeded with caution. He was expected to produce a new *opera buffa* as well as a full-scale grand opera, but they were long in coming. He was not going to be rushed into anything. The composer knew that he had to become more proficient in the French language, and in the French style, even to the extent of modifying his own style in composition.

Events conspired to throw a small spanner in the works when King Louis XVIII died six weeks after the Rossinis reached Paris and the composer was called upon to produce something suitable for the coronation of Charles X. He was not yet ready to deal with the French language and set an Italian text, written by the stage director at the Théâtre-Italien, *Il viaggio a Reims* (*The Journey to Rheims*, that being the city where French kings were crowned). It is usually described as a one-act opera but, since there is virtually no action at all, it is really more of a cantata. It was a hodgepodge of old and new music and included national songs from many countries – including 'God Save the King'. After two or three performances, Rossini reclaimed the score and refused to let anyone else have it despite some temptingly large offers. This was undoubtedly a wise move. The work, whose original form is now uncertain, was unlikely to add to his reputation, rather the reverse, while on the other hand it contained several fine pieces – a hunting song for example – worthy of a better vehicle, and a vehicle likely to run a lot longer and more profitably than a *pièce d'occasion* like *Il viaggio a Reims*.

Soon afterwards Rossini was laid up for several weeks with some unspecified illness, but he recovered in time to prepare a production of Meyerbeer's *Il crociato in Egitto*, first performed in Venice in 1824, at the Théâtre-Italien. He took a great deal of trouble with this, and it proved to be an inspired choice, if only because it brought Meyerbeer to Paris and the start of his meteoric French career. Rossini's fertilizing influence also explained the excellence of the singers, who included old friends like Ester Mombelli, Giuditta Pasta and the tenor Domenico Donzelli as well as others destined to be equally famous, notably the French bass, Nicolas-Prosper Levasseur.

The young composer,
Giacomo Meyerbeer. A
friend of Rossini's for
forty years (Mansell)

The peak of Meyerbeer's Parisian career was probably *Robert le diable*, first performed in 1831 and, though practically forgotten now, then one of the most spectacular successes in operatic history.

Rossini and Meyerbeer, who had first met in Venice in 1819, remained good and mutually admiring friends for forty years. This personal relationship says much for the character of the two men, Rossini especially, as there was much that might have disrupted it. In the early 1830s, one effect of Meyerbeer's success was to keep Rossini's operas almost entirely off the Parisian stage. Moreover, the demands of Meyerbeer on his singers were different from those of Rossini, hefty orchestration and huge choruses demanding volume and staying power above all. In some respects it was a return to the declamatory style, dismissed by one Italian listener as 'French shouting', which it had been Rossini's mission to refine. It must be said too that Meyerbeer's popularity was in some part due to the elaborate staging and scenic effects that were associated with the rise of grand opera. Chopin, writing home about an early performance of *Robert le diable*, described it as

> *a masterpiece of the new school, in which devils sing through speaking-trumpets and souls arise from graves ... in which there is a diorama in the theatre where at the end you see the interior of a church, the whole church, at Christmas or Easter, lighted up, with monks, with all the congregation on benches, with censers – even with the organ, the sound of which on the stage is enchanting and amazing and nearly drowns out the orchestra.*

In Paris early in 1825, Rossini was visited by Carl Maria von Weber, passing through on his way to London and already marked by the illness that would kill him there. Weber had written many harsh things about Rossini in the press, and was hesitant about calling on him at all. But Rossini did not bear professional grudges of that kind. He brushed aside Weber's halting attempts at apology for past criticism. He had never seen those articles, he insisted, as he could not read German. They should embrace and talk of other things. Weber himself was later to admit that their opposing aesthetics required him to condemn Rossini as the 'Lucifer of music', however good he might be judged in his own terms, and that he had once left a performance of *La Cenerentola* halfway through because he found he was 'beginning to like the stuff'!

The first Rossini production of his own work at the Théâtre-Italien, in October 1825, was that same opera. The occasion was notable also for the French debut of another brilliant singer, the tenor Giovanni Battista Rubini, later to captivate London as well as Paris. Rubini was also in the following productions, *La donna del lago* and *Otello*.

These works had already been performed in Paris, though not so well. In December came *Semiramide*, which had not been previously performed. The first night was marred by the breakdown of the *prima donna*, but after Pasta took over the part a month later the opera became a special favorite with the Parisians.

Standards at the Théâtre-Italien were certainly improving, but French audiences are even harder to satisfy than others, and Rossini, no stranger to unfair criticism, soon came under fire for providing nothing but Giacomo Meyerbeer or Rossini operas which were already familiar to the audience. The press accused him of being lazy and of doing what he liked regardless of obligations.

Attacks of this kind may have played a part in the renegotiating of Rossini's contract in October 1826 which ended his direct responsibility for the Théâtre-Italien. Instead he was given a handsome annual salary and the charming titles, *Premier Compositeur du Roi* and *Inspecteur Général du Chant en France*. The story goes that Rossini was sometimes observed listening to singers in the street and, when asked what he was doing, replied that he was carrying out his official duties as 'Inspector-General of Singing'. The titles were of course meaningless; they merely justified the salary, the purpose of the latter being to make sure Rossini stayed in France (late in 1826 Rossini was in fact considering an offer from the King's Theatre in London). Though no longer directly involved, he remained on good terms with later directors of the Italien and kept up a close interest in the affairs of that theater.

Rossini's works were still also appearing at the Odéon. One strange concoction was called *Ivanhoé*. It was a *pasticcio* of half a dozen of his operas, strung together and rearranged by the music publisher Antonio Pacini, with a new libretto based loosely on Sir Walter Scott's novel. The public seemed to like it, but some more solemn critics pondered the seemliness of the First Composer to the King giving his blessing to such a project.

It was not an isolated case either. Similar pastiches were scrambled together in other places, where attitudes were generally less reverent than they would be now. One arrangement by Castil-Blaze combined music by Rossini and Weber, of all people. Similarly, the quite common practice of performing single acts from two or three different operas, rather than a single complete work, would attract greater disapproval now than then, although, under the influence of the Romantic movement, attitudes were already changing. More people condemned infringements of the 'integrity of the work', but the feebleness of the copyright laws made it difficult for composers to mount effective protest against these practices even if they wished to do so.

By stages Rossini eased himself into his new role as a French composer. His first 'French' opera was a reworking of *Maometto II*, in three acts rather than the original two, which, cashing in on the popular cause of the Greek struggle for independence, became the politically correct *La Siège de Corinth*. It was first heard at the Salle le Peletier, the current home of the Opéra, in October 1826. One of the stars was the young French tenor, Adolphe Nourrit, a cultured, intelligent man with whom Rossini had a mutually beneficial relationship, each learning much from the other. Nourrit is one of the most interesting minor characters in the musical history of the time. Sadly, a victim of his own acute sensitivity, he was to end his own life at an early age.

La Siège de Corinth was received with great enthusiasm and remained extremely popular for several years, celebrating its one-hundredth performance in 1839 and remaining in the repertory for some years after that. 'Every number,' according to one paper's account of the first performance, was 'saluted by a triple salvo of applause.' A professor from the Conservatoire, not an institution that harbored many keen Rossinians, remarked that the composer had 'taken harmonic effects to such a degree of complication that one [may] ask if he has not made any further innovation impossible'. Rossini, summoned to the stage to receive the plaudits of his admirers, had to make an ostentatious exit after half an hour in order to persuade the audience to leave the theater. Led by musicians from the orchestra, many of them followed him back to his apartment in the Boulevard Montmartre.

Not everyone was pleased with the way things were developing. Carping critics complained about the sheer length of the new type of grand opera, and of the noisy orchestration. With a certain justice, it was said that the introduction of 'brass drum, trumpets, cracked brasses, etc.' which featured in the march in *Le Siège de Corinth* was basically un-Rossinian.

However, the same week Rossini was offered the distinction of the Légion d'Honneur. Tactfully, he declined on the grounds that French composers like Ferdinand Hérold – Rossini's inspired choice, incidentally, as voice coach at the Italien – had not yet been so recognized.

Rossini followed up *La Siège de Corinth* with a still greater success, *Moïse et Pharaon, ou Le Passage de la Mer Rouge*, in a new, French version, extended to four acts. Even previously hostile critics were won over, particularly by the singing, for by now Rossini had accomplished a minor revolution in banishing the Opéra's familiar declamatory style and restoring, if temporarily, true *bel canto*. The *Gazette* celebrated the end of 'French shouting'. From now on, it continued, 'they are going to sing at the Opéra as they sing at the [Théâtre-Italien]. *Vive* Rossini!'

Rossini was unable to take much pleasure from his triumph with *Moïse et Pharaon*. During rehearsals, he received a visit from a friend from Bologna, Dr. Gaetano Conti. He told him that his mother, Anna, who had long suffered heart problems, was gravely ill. Rossini's impulse was to rush off to Bologna immediately, but Dr. Conti reminded him of how his sudden arrival on an earlier occasion had over-excited his mother so much that she had been confined to bed for a week. Rossini accepted his warning and did not go. Anna died on February 20, 1827.

Rossini, an only child, had been a very good son. He was devoted to both parents, but his relationship with his mother was particularly intense: she was the person whom he loved above all others, including Colbran. There is no doubt that, like his father who could not bring himself to tell his son the dreadful news, he was devastated.

It is tempting to see Anna's death as marking a watershed in Rossini's life. The carefree, youthful genius was gone for good. Although he did not lose the capacity to enjoy himself, the future was more troubled – by bad health, bouts of depression and other problems of middle age.

A set design for La Siège de Corinth *(AKG)*

Guillaume Tell

After his mother's death Rossini had his father stay with him in Paris, sending a servant to accompany the grief-stricken old man from Bologna. Rossini himself talked more often of his desire to retire to Bologna, where the restoration of the palazzo he had bought six years before was at last nearing completion, but meanwhile his busy existence in Paris continued. It was social activity that still took up much of his time, and irritated those who felt he should be getting on with his promised opera. There were also occasional breaks, though a trip to the seaside at Dieppe with Isabella was not a success. Rossini was 'horribly bored'.

Whatever his critics might think, Rossini was working to fulfill his promise to write a truly original French opera. It was not the anticipated grand opera – he did not feel ready for that yet – but a comic opera, *Le Comte Ory*. The libretto was by the influential Eugene Scribe, from his one-act comedy based on a folk tale and now extended to two acts. Adolphe Nourrit, as well as giving some help with the writing, sang the title role.

Although there are elements of the old *opera buffa* tradition, including some earthy humor, *Le Comte Ory* is different in kind from the comic operas Rossini had composed ten years and more ago, before his liaison with Colbran diverted him into a more serious path. It lacks the vigorous comic drive of the *Barber*, for instance. Instead it has what Berlioz, hitherto a stern critic of Rossini, called 'a wealth of felicitous airs throughout'. Some of the music derived from *Il Viaggio a Reims*, though not the famous trio in Act II which Berlioz regarded as Rossini's masterpiece and others have described as worthy of Mozart at his best.

According to some accounts, the opera, sometimes described as *opéra-comique*, sometimes as *opéra bouffe* – we should perhaps describe it as an operetta – was not at first appreciated by the public as much as by more sophisticated listeners like Berlioz. However, the public turned up in sufficient numbers to make it a great success. It remained in the repertoire for about twenty years and was revived sporadically at the Opéra into the 1880s, attaining 443 performances altogether. It was never so popular in Italy, which may be an indication of how successfully Rossini had absorbed the Gallic spirit.

Alessandro Sanquirico's stage design for
Le Comte Ory *(Lebrecht)*

Rossini's Guillaume Tell *presented an idyllic portrait of country men and women whose actions were frequently heroic (Lebrecht)*

In addition to the profits accruing from performance, Rossini sold the publication rights to Eugène Troupenas for 16,000 francs. Troupenas had succeeded in breaking Rossini's resolution not to publish his scores for the first time with *La Siège de Corinthe*; thereafter he became a friend as well as Rossini's regular publisher.

Within a few days of the opening of *Le Comte Ory* in August 1828, Rossini left for the château of Petit-Bourg, a haven he had made use of before which belonged to his friend and patron, the aristocratic Spanish financier Alexandre Aguado, Marques de las Marismas. Rumor had it that the composer had withdrawn to work on his long-awaited grand opera, and on this occasion at least rumor was correct.

Rossini had already decided that the tale of the Swiss national hero should provide the subject of his French grand opera before he started work on *Le Comte Ory*, when he was shown a libretto by Étienne de Jouy based on Schiller's play *Wilhelm Tell*. He had previously rejected two librettos on different subjects by Eugène Scribe, both probably of superior quality (and both set later by other composers). No doubt the popular enthusiasm for the Greek struggle for independence against the Turks, for which Rossini had conducted a charity concert, and the success of his own *La Siège de Corinthe*, had inclined him favorably to stories of small nations fighting to be free. However, even Rossini could see that Jouy's libretto was far from adequate in its present state. It was much too long – more than 700 verses – and too ponderous and solemn. He called in a young poet, Hippolyte Bis, who virtually rewrote the second act while slimming down the other three. But Rossini, as he worked on it, found some further causes of dissatisfaction. The only source of literary assistance near at hand was his host's secretary, who provided, uncredited, some material in the second act.

On *Guillaume Tell* Rossini worked long and hard, probably longer than on any other opera. He admitted to spending five or six months on it, but the actual time was more as he had done some work before taking himself off to Petit-Bourg. In any case, while he would complain of tiredness and overwork when it suited him, he also liked to exaggerate his own facility. The story that the conspiracy scene in Act II (which Donizetti said had been written not by Rossini but by God) came to him while he was fishing, and ruined his sport through interfering with his concentration, should be taken, like many of Rossini's anecdotes about himself, with a grain of salt.

Rossini returned to Paris in October 1828, still with a good deal of scoring, and perhaps still some composition, to do. Since *Le Comte Ory*, he was the hero of the town and the press reports on the progress of the new opera suggest a fevered state of anticipation. Rehearsals would start on November 1. The score had been given to the copyist. It was an entirely new kind of music, the composer had promised 'no crescendos' ... Rossini had left town ... He was back again ... There were difficulties ...

The soprano Laure Cinti, who was to sing Mathilde, had recently married (she was henceforth known as Cinti-Damoreau) and had become inconveniently pregnant. An Austrian singer was hired to replace her, but she proved unsatisfactory. The opera was postponed (the composer was still in fact working on the score). Rehearsals at last began at the beginning of May 1829, with a July opening forecast. The date receded steadily: July 24, July 27. Cinti-Damoreau, now a mother, had a sore throat ...

The opera finally opened on August 3, before a highly distinguished audience.

Though the reaction of the audience, especially during the last two acts, was less than fervent, the response of virtually every critic was ecstatic. *Le Globe* heralded 'a new era, not only for French music, but for dramatic music in all countries'. In a sense that portentous judgment is justified. Grand opera was about to enter its most fruitful phase in France and Rossini contributed as much towards it as any single individual. If one evening were to be selected as the significant moment, then the first night of *Guillaume Tell* is as good as any.

Fellow composers without exception praised the opera in extravagant terms. Bellini said that, by comparison, all other contemporary composers were made to look like pygmies. Berlioz, distributing praise in terms as extravagant as those with which he had once cast blame, wrote a long and passionately enthusiastic article. Wagner was later to admit that some aspects of his own work were anticipated by *Guillaume Tell*, and Rossini's influence can indeed be detected here and there even in *The Ring*.

The public, for whom the opera was, as critics suggested at the time, a little too 'difficult' at first, gradually warmed to it, and it was performed at the Opéra more than forty times in the ten months between its opening and the July Revolution. After the *Barber*, it is probably Rossini's most famous opera today. Undoubtedly it contains some superb music, the best that Rossini ever wrote, but it is not an undisputed masterpiece. Some would say that, among Rossini's serious operas, it is challenged by *Semiramide* and perhaps *Tancredi*.

The libretto, described as a 'travesty' of Schiller's play, is not satisfactory. The characterization is perfunctory and the last two acts, in which very little action takes place, are dull. The libretto is partly to blame for a fault in *Guillaume Tell* that

*Mendelssohn
visited Rossini in
1835 and
reported that he
was 'big and
fat... amiable
and festive'
(Mansell)*

breaks a fundamental rule of drama: make the last act the best! The best act (of four) is Act II, and although there is some wonderful music to come, after the tremendous Act II finale there is a slight sense of anticlimax which is not completely redeemed until the final, thrilling climax.

Practically the only criticism made by Berlioz was that the opera was too long, a judgement shared by many others including the composer himself. Rossini in fact made some cuts after the first few performances, and three years later agreed to a three-act version produced at Bordeaux. Sheer length may have been one of the reasons for its relatively lukewarm reception by the public – lukewarm, at least, by comparison with the reception of *La Siège de Corinthe* or *Moïse et Pharaon*. Another technical problem was the tenor part, Arnold (Tell himself is a baritone). Someone described this role as a destroyer of voices, though far worse was to come. The admirable Nourrit was apparently unable to cope, in particular, with the fabulous aria 'Asile Héréditaire', which was therefore cut. When the role was taken over by Gilbert-Louis Duprez, famous for the wide range of his voice, in 1837, the opera took on a new lease of life.

Rossini's last opera soon became a feature of the international repertoire, though it was forced into some strange disguises. Since the villains are the Austrians, there were problems with the censors in Austrian-ruled territory. In Milan, the Austrians became English and the persecuted Swiss became the Scots; William Tell emerged in tartan as William Wallace. In other countries, local heroes were substituted, as it was thought that people found it difficult to get excited about the Swiss. Vienna itself was relatively liberal, and the opera was sung there in its original form. At the end, to prove they were still good Austrian patriots, the audience would give a cheer for the house of Habsburg.

Scots or Swiss, the opera was never very popular in Italy, and it gradually fell out of favor at the Opéra. It certainly could not compete with Meyerbeer's *Robert le diable*, first produced in 1831. Soon it was to be heard only in excerpts. Many years later, the director of the Opéra met Rossini in the street and, thinking he would be pleased, told him that Act II of *Guillaume Tell* was being performed that night. 'What?' said Rossini at his most sardonic, 'The whole act?'

Notoriously, Rossini's first French grand opera was also his last opera of any kind, and many explanations have been suggested for this once-prolific composer's cessation of activity in mid-career. It is usually the case that a creative artist continues to produce as long as he or she has the capacity to do so, and the cutting off of a career like Rossini's is put down to the drying up of the creative juices. It is true that Rossini had become less prolific in the 1820s than he was a decade earlier, but there is no reason to believe that after 1829 he ran out of steam. He simply did what he had long intended: he took voluntary early retirement.

Of course, he was out of sympathy with some contemporary musical developments, and may have thought of himself as belonging to an earlier age, but his decision to retire was not a sudden one. According to Stendhal, as early as 1819 Rossini, then twenty-eight, was talking of retiring at thirty. The death of his mother strengthened his desire to leave the turbulence of the operatic world and take life more gently in his Bologna palazzo – or so he wrote in letters to friends there. He told his father in 1827 that he wanted to go home for good in 1830, to 'act the gentleman and write what he wishes'. Nor, indeed, did he attempt to keep his plans secret. In April 1828 – four months before the opening of *Le Comte Ory* – the Paris publication *Revue musicale* reported:

> *Rossini has promised to write a work: Guillaume Tell, but he himself has asserted that he will not go beyond the promise that he has made; and that this opera will be the last to come from his pen.*

So it proved, though Rossini, whatever he said to *Le Globe*, would surely have been surprised if an angel had told him, as he journeyed home to Bologna with Isabella ten days after the first night of *Guillaume Tell*, that he really had written his last opera. He was, at that time, contracted to write several.

Certainly no one else believed that Rossini's career as as operatic composer was over. As time went by, and it gradually became clear that indeed it was over, the reasons naturally provoked a good deal of curiosity, and in later years Rossini was often asked to provide them.

He gave different answers, none wholly convincing. Lack of inspiration was one. In 1852 he told his friend Domenico Donzelli that

> *it was a sentiment of delicacy rather than vanity which led me to renounce money and fame {he had not exactly renounced them!}; otherwise I should not so soon have hung up my lyre on the wall. Music needs freshness of ideas; I am conscious of nothing but lassitude and crabbedness.*

However he was to tell another friend,

The facsimile of a musical piece written in 1858, the year the samedi soir tradition began (Mansell)

I wrote operas when melodies came in search of me, but, when I realized that the time had come for me to set out and look for them, I, in my well-known capacity as an idler, renounced the journey and ceased to write.

Two other factors which undoubtedly contributed to Rossini's creative silence during the second half of his life could not have been anticipated in the 1820s. One was the poor health that dogged him throughout his middle age. The other was his feeling that, in the musical sense if no other, he was out of tune with the times.

The beginnings of the Romantic era are usually ascribed to developments in German literature towards the end of the eighteenth century. However, the movement did not blossom in France and Italy until about 1830, the very time that Rossini ceased to write operas. Moreover, Romanticism remained more of a Northern than a Southern phenomenon. Italians are always loath to abandon their classical heritage – they never really embraced Gothic architecture either.

Although his subject matter was often Romantic, Rossini was not a Romantic composer. He had very little sympathy with most of the cultural changes characteristic of the age, and he had no liking for what became French grand opera, as typified by Meyerbeer's *Robert le diable* and subsequent works. A constant complaint of his later years was the decline of *bel canto*. People don't sing any more, he said, 'they scream, they bellow, they wrestle'. His main objection to Wagner's music was the threat which in Rossini's view it represented to vocal melody.

There is a great paradox in all this, since few people had done more than Rossini to prepare the way for the new style, and *Guillaume Tell* might well be regarded as almost the prototype of Romantic opera, with its nationalistic theme and its mountain setting. Perhaps that is why Rossini was unenthusiastic about it later; he spoke dismissively of its 'peasants, mountains and miseries', and he deliberately discouraged one attempted revival.

In later years Rossini more than once admitted that changing times and styles had put him off. In 1866 he told the composer Giovanni Pacini:

> {Music}, *which is based solely on sentiment and ideals, cannot escape the influence of the times we live in, and the sentiment and ideals of the present day are wholly concerned with steam* {a pet hate}, *rapine and barricades. Remember my philosophical determination to give up my Italian career in 1822, my French career in 1829. Such foresight is not vouchsafed to everybody; God granted it to me, and I have been grateful for it ever since.*

After an interval of some forty years, it was easy to assume motives and causes that were a good deal less clear at the time. It would be interesting to know exactly when Rossini himself squarely faced the fact that he had composed his last opera. Whatever he may have believed later, and whatever he may have said at the time, it is unlikely that this was as early as 1830.

A major reason for the succession of delays in the progress of *Guillaume Tell* towards its first performance was a dispute between Rossini and his employers. As a person and as a musician, Rossini was a genial, easy-going character, but one thing he took seriously was money, and in the pursuit of material advancement he could be extremely tough.

Early in 1827 Rossini was in communication with Rochefoucauld and other royal officials with a view to regularizing his somewhat peculiar official position. At this time Rossini was pining for Italy; despite his long stays in the city, he did not want to have to live in Paris permanently. He was also concerned, with good reason, that his position depended mainly on the goodwill of current officials (also the current monarch, though he may not, at that stage, have thought in those terms).

These negotiations dragged on for nearly two years.

In February 1829 Rossini brought matters to a head by proposing precise terms. He wanted a salary for life of 6,000 francs per annum, and three months' absence from Paris. In return, he would compose five operas in the next ten years (*Guillaume Tell* was to be the first of the five), for each of which he should be paid 15,000 francs, plus a benefit performance.

In themselves, these terms were apparently acceptable to the King and his ministers. However, those gentlemen were well aware of Rossini's desire, by this time widely published, to stop composing operas. They were naturally averse to paying him a salary for life if no future operas were forthcoming.

In flattering, courtly, not to say hypocritical language, flowery even by the standards of the time, Rossini piled on the pressure. Other countries had made more generous offers, he pointed out. It was not a question of self-interest, he was simply determined to contribute further to the glory of French music, etc. Still the contract failed to materialize. Rossini was getting irritable. He warned the Opéra's director that, unless it did, he would stop rehearsals of *Guillaume Tell* and withold the score for the final act, which had not yet reached the copyist. In due course, he did indeed call off rehearsals.

This forced the director, Émile Lubbert, to enter the lists in Rossini's support.

Rochefoucauld consulted his minister, his minister probably consulted the King. It is not clear what was holding things up: there must have been some opposition to Rossini somewhere in the Court. Anyhow, at last the contract, signed by the King personally, was delivered, and rehearsals were resumed.

Olympe Pèlissier, a professional courtesan and Rossini's second wife (Lebrecht)

Changing Times

The Rossinis traveled to Bologna by way of Milan, where they met Bellini, twenty-eight years old and the very picture of a Romantic artist. Rossini took to him, and was to give him much valuable advice, particularly in connection with his Parisian opera, *I Puritani di Scozia* (1835), which, due to Bellini's early death, proved to be sadly his last.

A spell playing the country gentleman at Castenaso was cut short by the early onset of winter, prompting a move to the greater comfort of Rossini's palazzo in town. He took a close interest in the affairs of the Teatro Communale, and lured Giuditta Pasta to appear there.

The July Revolution of 1830 seemed to threaten Rossini's congenial arrangements in Paris. He returned to the city in September and found his fears realized: his contract had been canceled. Though he was not sorry to be free of the obligation to compose four more works for the Opéra, he was not going to give up his annuity without a fight. Forced to go to law, it was over five years before he finally won his case.

In all this he had invaluable support from the rich and clever Aguado, who not only provided free board and lodging but, no doubt, useful advice as well. Aguado took him off to Madrid in 1831, where he was subject to the usual flattering attention and, as in England, indulged in some rather comical music-making with the monarch.

The price for his Spanish holiday was to obey the request of an eminent

A *contemporary cartoon of Rossini surrounded by his creations (Lebrecht)*

I. R. TEATRO ALLA SCALA.

In questa sera di Sabbato **24 Maggio 1834** si darà L'ULTIMA RECITA
DI MAD. MALIBRAN coll' Opera

OTELLO
OSSIA
IL MORO DI VENEZIA

Musica del Maestro Cavaliere sig. GIOACCHINO ROSSINI.

PERSONAGGI

DESDÈMONA . : . .	Signore	MALIBRAN MARIA.
EMILIA	„	BAYLLOU FELICITA.
RODRIGO	„	GARCIA RUEZ.
OTELLO	Signori	REINA DOMENICO.
ÈLMIRO	„	MARINI IGNAZIO.
JAGO	„	BALFE GUGLIELMO.
DOGE	„	MARCONI NAPOLEONE.

Dopo il primo atto, essendo indisposto tuttora il sig. *Priora*, avrà luogo un
PASSO A QUATTRO fra le allieve dell' I. R. Accademia, signore *Ancement*,
Ciocca, *Romagnoli* e *Zambelli*.

Prezzo del Biglietto { Al Teatro . . . lir. **6**
{ Al Loggione . . . „ **2** } austriache.
Per una Sedia chiusa „ **15**

Daranno accesso alle File chiuse due ingressi a dritta e sinistra nell' atrio
del suddetto Teatro. - Ciascun concorrente conserva il Biglietto a ga-
ranzia del posto.
Al Camerino si affittano Palchi di quinta Fila.

Lo Spettacolo incomincierà alle ore otto e mezzo.

Milano 2 24 Maggio 1834.   *Tipografia Pirola*

*The announcement
of a performance of
Otello at La
Scala, Milan,
featuring one of
Rossini's favorite
singers, Maria
Malibran
(Lebrecht)*

ecclesiastical friend of Aguado to write for him a Stabat Mater (a devotional poem used in Roman Catholic liturgy). Rossini was not keen to comply; he had once sworn never to set those words because Pergolesi had done it so beautifully over one hundred years before. Still, he kept his promise although, back in Paris, he hired a musician called Giovanni Tadolini to help him complete it.

The Spanish bishop for whom the work was written promised not to let it out of his possession, but after his death in 1837 his executors sold it to a Paris publisher who sought Rossini's permission to publish. Declining, Rossini pointed out that, first, the copyright belonged to him, not to the heirs of the bishop, and that a good part of the music had not been written by him at all. Another complicated legal dispute began. The business seems to have galvanized him into finishing the work (he said he had done so earlier but that seems doubtful), so that a complete and 'unghosted' work could be published by his own publisher, Troupenas.

Rossini's Stabat Mater was first performed in Paris in 1842. A few months later Rossini heard it for the first time in Bologna, where it was conducted by Donizetti, the composer himself being too ill. The work, clearly influenced by Pergolesi, has found many admirers. Though not unreverential, the music is attractively brisk and unashamedly dramatic.

In the course of his travels around France, in 1832 Rossini met, possibly not for the first time, Olympe Pélissier, a professional courtesan since her very early youth, but equipped with the heart of gold often associated with that profession as well as, since the death of her last lover, a sizable independent income. She also had a refreshingly frank way of speaking. Five years his junior, she and Rossini hit it off immediately.

Essentially, Rossini, whose health had begun to deteriorate by 1832, needed mothering, and this Olympe was both willing and able to undertake. Though there was no divorce in Italy, the Rossini marriage had failed long ago. Isabella had developed extravagant habits in Paris, and was now consigned to Bologna under the aged eye of her father-in-law. He sent off critical reports about her, at first fairly moderate in tone but becoming increasingly outraged as time went by. To apportion blame would be otiose, but Isabella, like other great stars finding retirement difficult to cope with, does seem to have gone off the rails in her later years. At first she made some effort to accept Olympe, but inevitably they soon quarreled, and after an official separation was formalized in 1837 little contact took place between Rossini and his wife until her final illness in 1845. After her death, at nearly sixty, Rossini was at last free to marry Olympe, which he did nearly a year later.

Rossini himself returned to Bologna in the summer of 1834 in an effort to recover his health which, with ups and downs, had been getting steadily worse. There seems to be general agreement that his chief physical ailment was venereal in origin. Besides that he had always had neurotic tendencies; now even the smallest stresses and strains left him exhausted, and he was growing increasingly subject to both anxiety attacks and fits of depression.

He was not entirely idle during these years, however. He took a close and active interest in the Théâtre-Italien, now at the peak of its reputation, and he wrote a good deal of vocal music, a collection of which was published by Troupenas in 1835 as *Soirées musicales*. Much of this was written for Paris concert parties, where Rossini made a good deal of money, often accompanying the multi-talented soprano Malibran to whom he was greatly attached. For her he wrote in 1832 the cantata

Felix Mendelssohn (right) and Franz Liszt (top) were just two of the remarkably eminent visitors Rossini received towards the end of his life (AKG)

*Rossini's passport issued by
the 'Governo Pontificio' for a
journey to Paris (Lebrecht)*

'*Giovanna d'Arco*' ('*Joan of Arc*'), and he paid a heartfelt tribute to her, 'most marvellous of them all', when, sadly, she died at the age of twenty-eight in 1836.

The legal dispute over his annuity kept Rossini in Paris most of the time until it was settled in his favor in December 1835 but, partly because of and partly in spite of his poor health, he led a somewhat peripatetic existence in the 1830s. Often, though not always, he was accompanied by Olympe; some hostesses refused to receive her. In 1835 he was in Germany, where he met Mendelssohn, who played for him. Mendelssohn reported to his family that Rossini was 'big and fat [and] in his most amiable and festive mood! Truly, I know few men who can be as spirited and amusing as Rossini when he wants to be. And we did nothing but laugh'.

About this time Rossini made his first train journey. It was worse than a ship – uncomfortable and noisy, jerking and jolting – and he refused to travel by rail ever again. He placed steam along with 'rapine and barricades' among the greatest evils of the age.

In 1838, when it had become too awkward to live in Bologna with Olympe, they settled for a time in Milan. There Rossini gained some reputation as an after-dinner host, a foretaste of the famous Saturday-night *soirées* in Paris in his later years. One of his callers was Liszt, who reported: 'Rossini [has] become rich, idle and illustrious'.

Joyful times were, however, infrequent. Further health troubles materialized in 1838, a year of disasters. The Théâtre-Italien was burned down; its director, Rossini's friend Carlo Severini, died in the flames. Adolphe Nourrit ended his life in that year and Rossini's father died soon after celebrating his eightieth birthday in November.

Rossini, as Liszt observed, was doing little composing at this period; but he did not lose touch with the musical world and had several particular interests, such as the career of his protégé Nicolai Ivanov, a Russian tenor. From 1839, though holding only an honorary post, he was closely involved with the affairs of the Liceo in Bologna, where with the loyalty to his friends that was one of his many attractive characteristics, he worked harder than he had when running the Théâtre-Italien. Among other useful innovations, he organized regular concerts featuring composers such as Mendelssohn and Weber, for he kept in touch with musical development in Germany too. His efforts to lure Donizetti to Bologna as director of the Liceo were, however, unsuccessful – in spite of his considerable powers of persuasion and Donizetti's respect and affection for him. Remarking that Bologna was 'sad', Donizetti accepted an appointment in Vienna instead.

Another visitor to Bologna in 1842 was Verdi, then aged twenty-nine. Rossini had attended the first performance of his *Nabucco* at La Scala in Milan. It was a tremendous success and restored Verdi's faith in composition, which he had renounced after the tragic deaths of his wife and two children all within two years. Rossini's attitude towards this new young lion was admiring though guarded. Verdi reported to a friend:

> *I went to visit Rossini, who greeted me very politely, and the welcome seemed to me sincere. However that may be, I was very pleased. When I think that the reputation alive throughout the world is Rossini, I could kill myself, and with me all the imbeciles. Oh, it's a great thing to be Rossini!*

Rossini himself would doubtless have disagreed. However, his health had taken – only temporarily as it proved – a turn for the better after Olympe had dragged him

Paris: the Boulevard des Italiens where the Rossinis had an apartment (AKG)

to Paris for treatment by a noted physician, Jean Civiale. The visit lasted four months. The doctor insisted on virtual isolation, fiercely enforced by the devoted Olympe, for three months, but in the remaining month Rossini is said to have received 2,000 visitors!

In 1848, Europe's 'year of revolutions', political turmoil rocked the Continent. The Bolognese, though they had recently acquired a less reactionary ruler in Pope Pio Nono (Pius IX), rallied to the cause of Italian independence. Rossini, sympathetic to reform but in general a political innocent, did not care for the rough revolutionary spirit. Although he did set some patriotic verses to music, his coolness was known. On one occasion he was hooted at in the streets and denounced as a rich reactionary. Alarmed, he and Olympe fled to Florence. News of fighting in Bologna did nothing to hasten their return, which did not take place until l850, after the revolution had collapsed along with the republic briefly established by Mazzini and his followers in Rome.

Unfortunately Rossini again angered his fellow citizens by openly associating with the hated Austrians, and the unpleasant atmosphere in the city forced him back to Florence in 1851. Furnishings from his palazzo followed him in crates – with a military escort! Florence was culturally and socially more congenial and, whether he knew it or not, Rossini had left the city which for so long he had considered his home for the last time.

Though for different reasons, life in Florence was no happier. The composer's health worsened again, and there were fears for his sanity. Donizetti had become insane as a result of syphilis before his death in 1848, and rumors that Rossini too had lost his mind had to be publicly denied by Olympe. Rossini referred to himself as 'the father of all those who suffer from nervous trouble', and he envied creatures who had no feelings, especially animals. (Perhaps he was thinking of the dog to which Olympe was devoted, described by one disgusted visitor compelled to nurse it on his lap as a 'stinking beast'.)

Another visitor, who saw Rossini at his worst, reported:

Rossini truly was sick, disturbed, nervous, very much weakened and depressed in spirit ... The conversation turned on nothing but the discomforts that he suffered or imagined that he suffered ... {He} moved around the room with agitated steps, struck his head, and, fulminating against his adverse fate, exclaimed: 'Someone else in my state would kill himself, but I ...haven't the courage ...'

The piano stood, dusty and neglected, in the corner. The devotion of Olympe, who at times was near the end of her tether, just about kept him going.

As he did not get better, Olympe decided that they should move back to Paris, where the best medical treatment was to be had. They left in the spring of 1855, traveling slowly by road. Rossini had seen the last of his native land.

Finale

When Rossini returned to Paris in 1855 he was sixty-three years old and a frail old man. Since his health had been intermittently bad for over twenty years, his prospects were not good. But, miraculously, he was to experience a personal renaissance. As sometimes happens to those plagued by illness in middle life, in old age Rossini regained, for well over a decade, his fitness, his plumpness, his enjoyment of food and his sense of humor.

It did not happen all at once. When the news that he had returned to Paris got out, hundreds of people wanted to see him, but most of them had to be turned away. He was too feeble to receive hordes of admirers. However, in June he told Verdi, who was in Paris for the opening of *Les Vêpres siciliennes*, 'You don't know in what a prison I've been confined,' significantly using the past tense.

Rossini was immensely famous and also very sociable; as a result there are numerous accounts of him in his last period, by friends and by visiting musicians, such as Wagner, who was spurred on to visit him, in spite of inaccurate press stories of Rossini's hostility, by his keen curiosity over Rossini's abnegation of his art. This wealth of information, though welcome, is unfortunately in marked contrast to the sources for his early years, when he was composing his operas.

The Rossinis lived in spacious apartments in the Chausée d'Antin near the corner of the Boulevard des Italiens. During the summer they moved out to a villa in Passy. They were offered one rent-free by the city, but Rossini preferred to build his own. It was not begun until 1859, when the composer was already sixty-seven, showing a

Despite his longing to return to Italy, Rossini lived in Paris from 1855 to his death in 1868 (AKG)

degree of optimism about longevity. It had a gilded lyre on the front gate to indicate that Rossini was in residence, and its flowerbeds were made in the shapes of musical instruments.

Rossini began composing again early in 1857, songs and slight instrumental works which were collected as *Péchés de vieillesse* (*Sins of Old Age*). They include songs of some felicity as well as some jokey or satirical works – a take-off of Offenbach for one finger on the piano, for example.

Rossini's wit, fully restored, could be deadly, as numerous anecdotes – not all, perhaps, of unimpeachable authenticity – attest. Verdi, who was said to have been a marvelous mimic of Rossini's manner, reported an incident that occurred soon after the death of Rossini's old friend and admirer Meyerbeer in 1864. Rossini received a visit from the late composer's nephew, who had written a funeral march for his uncle. The young man played the piece on the piano, with Rossini listening solemnly. 'Very good, very good!' he exclaimed at the end. 'But, truthfully, wouldn't it have been better if you had died and your poor uncle had composed the march?'

Rossini liked order, and in his sixties the pattern of his daily life scarcely varied. He rose at eight and breakfasted on a roll and coffee – later, sometimes eggs with a glass of claret – while Olympe opened the mail. He received visitors for an hour or so, before going for a walk, weather permitting, during which he might do some shopping for Olympe, or call on rich friends like the Rothschilds. On fine days he might take a cab to the Bois de Boulogne and stroll among the trees. He returned home at about one, took a glass of wine but apparently ate no lunch, saving up for the main meal of the day at six in the evening. Food was generally simple but good, enhanced by specialities – Stilton cheese for example – sent by friends and

Rossini on his deathbed by Gustav Doré, an occasional attendant of the Samedi soir (Lebrecht)

acquaintances abroad. The Rossinis seldom dined out.

After dinner he had a brief nap, then listened as Olympe read items from the newspaper. Very close friends might drop in for a chat later, and Rossini might play the piano, chiefly his old favorites, Haydn and Mozart. (Once a visitor asked him which was his best opera: *'Don Giovanni,'* was the instant reply.) Anyone who had not left by ten received a gentle hint that it was time to go.

Samedi soir – Saturday evening – was different. Then, up to sixteen people would be invited to dinner, and many more would arrive, also by formal invitation, afterwards, when the musical program, designed by Rossini but including other people's music besides his own, began. These evenings became a famous social institution in Paris. They were attended by almost every figure of note in the international musical world: Auber, Bizet, Arrigo Boito, Gounod, Liszt, Meyerbeer, the young Saint-Saëns, Verdi, to name only a few composers. Some works received their first performance at a Rossini *Samedi soir*. Nor was the distinguished company confined to musicians. The artist Gustave Doré, who admittedly also had a fine singing voice, attended some of the later 'Saturday evenings'.

On these occasions Rossini might play the piano, even sing, but mostly he played

only the benign and charming host. Public appearances were few. He sometimes attended a rehearsal at the Paris Opéra, if the work concerned was by one of his friends, but he refused to become involved in productions of even his own works. The appearance of two marvelous Italian singers in the old *bel canto* tradition, the Marchisio sisters from Turin, revivified Rossini operas, especially *Semiramide*, in Italy, and these splendid girls were almost enough to tempt him back into operatic composition. 'My dear children,' he greeted them, 'you have brought a dead man back to life!'

They were probably at least partly responsible for Rossini's last major composition, which was, fittingly no doubt, a mass. He called it, in his ironical, self-deprecatory way, 'Petite messe solennelle', though it is certainly not small and, while closer to traditional Church music than the Stabat Mater, not particularly solemn either. It was written during the summer of 1863, when the composer was seventy-one, in fourteen sections, for four solo voices and chorus, accompanied by two pianos and harmonium. Francis Toye considered it 'an exceedingly fine work, in one sense the most successful of all Rossini's serious compositions'. Contemporaries were more ecstatic. The music would melt the stones of a cathedral, wrote one critic. Others pointed out the originality of the harmonization, which prompted Rossini's explanation, 'I didn't spare the dissonances, but I put some sugar in too.'

When asked if he were going to orchestrate his mass, Rossini, who had been rather grumpy while composing it and was exhausted afterwards, at first denied any

The funeral of Rossini in Paris drew a huge crowd of mourners (Mansell)

such intention. However, if he did not orchestrate it, someone else would, probably not to his liking, so he undertook the task in 1866. The full score runs to nearly five hundred manuscript pages.

Besides the 'Petite messe solennelle', he wrote some minor pieces in his last years. Among them were a hymn to Napoleon III, performed with an orchestra of 800 players, a military fanfare that included saxophones, and – his one setting of English words – a hymn for the Birmingham Festival of 1867.

At the age of seventy, Rossini was said to look at least ten years younger. He still took a great interest in food and flirted with young women. The painter, Cesarino de Sanctis, who painted his portrait in 1862, left a vivid account of him,

*round-shouldered, his paunch protruding, as he moved about the salon with short steps, doing with much simplicity the honours of the house. From his looks, one would not have judged him to be an artist and one of the greatest geniuses of our time. The reddish-blond wig {*Rossini lost his hair early and possessed a multitude of what someone described as very 'wiggy' wigs*} that crudely outlined his forehead and temples contrasted strangely with his rather pallid and meticulously shaved face. His powerful imagination was evidenced only by his vivacious and penetrating eyes, just as one divined from his lips, thin and shaped slightly towards the sardonic, that he was a man of uncommon intelligence. There was not a trace of arrogance in him, or of that heavy manner which people of great fame not rarely take on.*

Nevertheless, in his seventies Rossini inevitably grew less robust. He suffered chest and other troubles during the winters, and in December 1866 he had what was probably a slight stroke. By February 28, when he celebrated his seventy-fifth birthday, he had completely recovered, but the following winter he was again ill, this time with a return of the psychological symptoms which had dogged him in his forties and fifties. He was forced to take life very quietly.

Spring brought little improvement. He was well enough for the *Samedi soirs* to resume at Passy, but when October came, he was too frail to move back to town. It became clear that he was now also suffering from what was presumably rectal cancer. He survived two operations, but he was a dying man, and in his last days suffered much pain and distress, relieved occasionally by flashes of the old Rossini – rebuking the Virgin Mary for failing to relieve his pain. He died on Friday, November 13, 1868.

Rossini's tomb in Santa Croce, Florence, photographed in 1900 (AKG)

rossini

the complete works

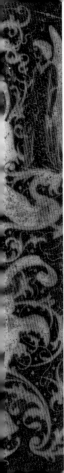

Rossini did not number his works. They are listed here by category and dates are given where known. Some of the works attributed to Rossini are now thought to be of doubtful authorship and they are not included in the following list.

OPERAS

Demetrio e Polibio, dramma serio (before 1808)

La cambiale di matrimonio, farsa comica (1810)

L'equivoco stravagante, dramma giocoso (1811)

L'inganno felice, farsa (1812)

Ciro in Babilonia, ossia La caduta de Baldassare, dramma con cori (1812)

La scala di seta, farsa comica (1812)

La pietra del paragone, melodramma giocoso (1812)

L'occasione fa il ladro, burletta (1812)

Il Signor Bruschino, ossia Il figlio per azzardo, farsa giocosa (1813)

Tancredi, melodramma eroico (1813)

L'Italiana in Algeri, dramma giocoso (1813)

Aureliano in Palmira, dramma serio (1813)

Il Turco in Italia, dramma buffo (1814)

Sigismondo, dramma (1814)

Elisabetta, regina d'Inghilterra, dramma (1815)

Torvaldo e Dorliska, dramma semiserio (1815)

*Il barbiere di Siviglia (originally Almaviva, ossia l'inutile precauzione),
commedia* (1816)

La gazzetta, dramma/opera buffa (1816)

Otello, ossia Il moro di Venezia, dramma (1816)

La Cenerentola, ossia La bontà in trionfo, dramma giocoso (1817)

La gazza ladra, melodramma (1817)

Armida, dramma (1817)

Adelaide di Borgogna, dramma (1817)

Mosè in Egitto, azione tragico-sacra (1818; Act 3, rev. March 1819)

Adina, farsa (1818)

Ricciardo e Zoraide, dramma (1818)

Ermione, azione tragica (1819)

Eduardo e Cristina, dramma (1819)

La donna del lago, melodramma (1819)

Bianca e Falliero, ossia Il consiglio dei tre; melodramma (1819)

Maometto II, dramma (1820)

Matilde (di) Shabran, ossia Bellezza, e cuor di ferro, melodramma giocoso (1821)

Zelmira, dramma (1822)

Semiramide, melodramma tragico (1823)

Il viaggio a Reims, ossia L'albergo del giglio d'oro, dramma giocoso (1825)

Le Siège de Corinthe [rev. of *Maometto II*], *tragédie-lyrique* (1826)

Moïse et Pharaon, ou Le passage de la Mer Rouge [*rev. of Mosè in Egitto*], *opéra* (1827)

Le Comte Ory, opéra/opéra-comique (1828)

Guillaume Tell, opéra (1829)

Works derived from Rossini operas with the composer's participation.

Ivanhoé, adapted by A. Pacini (1826)

Robert Bruce, adapted by L. A. Niedermeyer (1846)

INCIDENTAL MUSIC

Edipo a Colono, music for Sophocles' Oedipus at Colonus (before 1817)

RELIGIOUS MUSIC

Kyrie a tre voci; Gloria; Laudamus; Gratias; Domine Deus; Qui tollis; Laudamus and *Qui tollis; Quoniam; Crucifixus; Dixit; De torrente; Gloria Patri; Sicut erat;* Magnificat. *Messa*: Christe eleison; Benedicta et venerabilis; Qui tollis; Qui sedes. *Messa*: Kyrie, Gloria, Credo. *Messa*: Kyrie, Gloria, Credo. *Messa* (1802–9)

Quoniam (1813)

Messa di Gloria (1820)

Preghiera: 'Deh tu pietoso cielo' (c.1820)

Tantum ergo (1824)

Stabat Mater (1832) nos. 1, 5–9 by Rossini, nos. 2–4, 10–12 by Tadolini (2nd version, 1841) 10 nos. all by Rossini.

Trois choeurs religieux: 1. La foi (P. Goubaux); 2. L'espérance (H. Lucas); 3. La charité (L. Colet) (1844)

Tantum ergo (1847)

O salutaris hostia (1857)

Laus Deo (1861)

'Petite messe solennelle' (1864) 2nd version with orchestral
accompaniment, 1867

CANTATAS

Il pianto d'Armonia sulla morte di Orfeo (1808)

La morte di Didone (1818)

Dalle quete e pallid'ombre (1812)

Egle ed Irene (1814)

L'Aurora (1815)

Le nozze di Teti e di Peleo (1816)

Omaggio umiliato (1819)

Cantata (1819)

La riconoscenza (1821)

Giunone (before 1822)

La Santa Alleanza (1822)

Il vero omaggio (1822)

Omaggio pastorale (1823)

Il pianto delle muse in morte di Lord Byron (1824)

Cantata per il battesimo del figlio del banchiere Aguado (1827)

L'armonica cetra del nume (1830)

Giovanna d'Arco (1832. Rev. 1852)

Cantatina (1832)

Cantata in honore del Sommo Pontefice Pio Nono (1847)

CHORUSES, HYMNS

'Inno dell'Indipendenza' ('Sorgi, Italia, venuta è già l'ora'), hymn
(1815)

De l'Italie et de la France, hymn (1825)

Santo Genio dell'Italia terra, chorus (1844)

Su fratelli, letizia si canti, chorus (1846)

Segna Iddio ne' suoi confini, chorus (1848)

È foriera la Pace ai mortali, hymn (1850)

Hymne à Napoléon III et à son Vaillant Peuple
('Dieu tout puissant'), chorus (1867)

VOCAL MUSIC

Se il vuol la molinara (1801)

Dolce aurette che spirate (1810)

La mia pace io già perdei (1812)

Quai voce, quae note (1833)

Alla voce della gloria (1833)

Amore mi assisti (c. 1814)

Three pieces for Giuseppe Nicolini's *Quinto Fabio*, (1817)
1. Coro e cavatina 'Cara Patria, invitta Roma'
2. Aria 'Guido Marte i nostri passi'
3. (possibly not by Rossini) Duet 'Ah! per pietà t'arresta' (1817)

Il trovatore ('Chi m'ascolta il canto usato') (1818)

Il Carnevale di Venezia ('Siamo ciechi, siamo nati') (1821)

Beltà crudele ('Amori scendete propizi al mio core') (1821)

La pastorella ('Odia la pastorella') (c. 1821)

Canzonetta Spagnuola ('En medio a mis dolores' or 'Piangea un dì pensando') (1821)

Infelice ch'io son (1821)

Addio ai viennesi ('Da voi parto, amate sponde') (1822)

Dall'Oriente l'astro del giorno (1824)

Ridiamo, cantiamo, che tutto sen va (1824)

In giorno sì bello (1824)

Tre Quartetti da Camera 1. not traced 2. 'In giorno sì bello'

3. 'Oh giorno sereno' (1827)

Les adieux à Rome ('Rome pour la dernière fois') (1827)

Orage et beau temps ('Sur les flots inconstants') (c. 1829–30)

La passeggiata ('Or che di fiori adorno') (1831)

La dichiarazuine ('Ch'io mai vi possa lasciar d'amare') (c.1834)

Les soirées musicales (c. 1830–35)

1. La promessa ('Ch'io mai vi possa lasciar d'amare')
2. Il rimprovero ('Mi lagnerò tacendo')
3. La partenza ('Ecco quel fiero istante')
4. L'orgia ('Amiamo, cantiamo')
5. L'invito ('Vieni o Ruggiero')
6. La pastorella dell'Alpi ('Son bella pastorella')
7. La gita in gondola ('Voli l'agile barchetta')
8. La danza ('Già la luna è in mezzo al mare')
9. La regata veneziana ('Voga o Tonio benedetto')
10. La pesca ('Già la notte s'avvicina')
11. La serenata ('Mira, la bianca luna')
12. Li marinari ('Marinaro in guardia stà')

Deux nocturnes (Crével de Charlemagne) (1836)

1 Adieu à l'Italie ('Je te quitte, belle Italie')
2. Le départ ('Il faut partir')

Nizza ('Mi lagnerò tacendo', 'Nizza, je puis sans peine') (1836)

L'âme délaisée ('Mon bien aimé') (1844)

Francesca da Rimini ('Farò come colui che piange e dice') (1848)

Mi lagnerò tascendo (c. 1858)

INSTRUMENTAL

Six *Sonate a quattro* in G major, A major, C major, B♭ major, E♭ major, D major (1804)

Overture *al conventello*, D major (c. 1806)

Five duets, E♭ major, E♭ major, B♭ major, E♭ major, E♭ major (c. 1806)

Overture, D major (1808)

Overture, E♭ major, (1809)

Overture *obbligata a contrabasso*, D major (c. 1807–10)

Variazioni a più istrumenti obbligati, F major (1809)

Variazioni di clarinetto, C major (1809)

Andante e Tema con variazioni, F major (1812)

Andante e Tema con variazioni per arpa e violino, F major (c. 1820)

Passo doppio (1822)

Waltz, E♭ major (1823)

Serenata, E♭ major (1823)

Duetto, D major (1824)

Rendez-vous de chasse, D major (1828)

Fantasie, E♭ major (1829)

Three Military Marches, G major, E♭ major, E♭ major (1837)

Scherzo, A minor (1843, rev. 1850)

Tema originale di Rossini variato per violino da Giovacchino Giovacchini, A major (1845)

March ('Pas-redoublé'), C major (1852)

Thème de Rossini suivi de deux variations et coda par Moscheles Père, E major (1860)

La corona d'Italia, E♭ major (1868)

PÉCHÉS DE VIEILLESSE (1857–68)

VOL.I ALBUM ITALIANO

1. I gondolieri
2. La lontananza, arietta
3. Bolero 'Tirana alla spagnola', 'Mi lagnerò tacendo'
4. L'ultimo ricordo, elegia
5. La fioraja fiorentina ('I più bei fior comprate'), arietta
6. Le gittane
7. Ave Maria ('A te, che benedetta'), aria
8–10. LA REGATA VENEZIANA, THREE CANZONETTAS
8. Anzoleta avanti la regata ('Là su la machina'). French version, barcarolle, 'Plus de vent perfide'.
9. Anzoleta co passa la regata ('Ixe qua vardeli povereti').
10. Anzoleta dopo la regata ('Ciapa un baso').
11. Il fanciullo smarrito ('Oh! chi avesse trovato un fanciulletto')
12. La passeggiata

VOL.II ALBUM FRANÇAIS

1. Toast pour le nouvel an ('En ce jour si doux')

2. Roméo ('Juliette chère idole')

3. Pompadour, la grande coquette

4. Un sou. Complainte à deux voix ('Pitié pour la misère')

5. Chanson de Zora, La petite Bohémienne ('Gens de la plaine')

6. La nuit de Noël ('Calme et sans voile'). Italian version
'Tu che a salvarci'.

7. Le dodo des enfants ('Mon fils, rose éphémère')

8. Le Lazzarone. Chansonette de Cabaret ('au bord des flots a'Azur')

9. Adieux à la vie. Élégie sur une seule note
('Salut! dernière aurore')

10. Soupirs et sourires, Nocturne ('Dans le sentier des Roses')

11. L'orphéline du Tyrol, Ballade élégie ('Seule, une pauvre enfant')

12. Choeur de chasseurs démocrates ('En chasse amis, en chasse')

VOL.III MORCEAUX RÉSERVÉS

1. Quelques mesures de chant funèbre: à mon pauvre ami Meyerbeer ('Pleure, pleure, muse sublime')

2. L'Esule ('Qui sempre ride in cielo')

3. Les amants de Séville, Tirana pour deux voix ('Loin de votre Séville')

4. Ave Maria ('Ave Maria gratia plena')

5. L'amour à Pékin: melodie sur la gamme chinoise ('Mon coeur blessé')

6. Le chant des Titans ('Guerre! Massacre! Carnage!')

7. Preghiera ('Tu che di verde il prato')

8. Au chevet d'un mourant, Élégie ('De la douleur naît l'espérance')

9. Le sylvain, ('Belles Nymphes blondes')

10. Cantemus Domino, imitazione ad otto voci reali

11. Ariette à l'ancienne ('Que le jour me dure')

12. Le départ des promis, Tyrolienne sentimentale ('L'honneur appelle')

VOLS IV—VIII

'A little of everything. A collection of 56 semi-comical piano pieces.' Rossini.

VOL.IV QUATRE MENDIANTS ET QUATRE HORS D'OEUVRES

Quatre mediants:
1. Les figues sèches, D major
2. Les amandes, G major
3. Les raisins, C major
4. Les noisettes, B minor

Quatre hors d'oeuvres:
1. Les radis, A minor
2. Les anchois, D major
3. Les cornichons, E major
4. Le beurre, B♭ major

VOL.V ALBUM POUR LES ENFANTS ADOLESCENTS

1. Première Communion, E♭ major
2. Thème naïf et variations idem, G major
3. Saltarello à l'italienne, A♭ major
4. Prélude moresque, E minor
5. Valse lugubre, C major
6. Impromptu anodin, E♭ major
7. L'innocence italienne; La candeur française, A minor, A major
8. Prélude convulsif, C major
9. La lagune de Venise à l'expiration de l'anée 1861!!! G♭ major
10. Ouf! les petits pois, B major
11. Un sauté, D major
12. Hachis romantique, A minor

VOL. VI ALBUM POUR LES ENFANTS DÉGOURDIS

1. Mon prélude hygiénique du matin, C major
2. Prélude baroque, A minor
3. Memento homo, C minor
4. Assez de memento: dansons, F major
5. La pesarese, B♭ major
6. Valse torturée, D major
7. Une caresse à ma femme, G major
8. Barcarole, E♭ major
9. Un petit train de plaisir comico-imitatif, C major
10. Fausse couche de polka-mazurka, A♭ major
11. Étude asthmatique, E major
12. Un enterrement en Carnaval, D major

VOL. VII ALBUM DE CHAUMIÈRE

1. Gymnastique d'écartement, A♭ major
2. Prélude fugassé, E major
3. Petite polka chinoise, B minor
4. Petite valse de boudoir, A♭ major
5. Prélude inoffensif, C major
6. Petite valse, 'L'huile de Ricin', E major
7. Un profond sommeil; Un reveil en sursaut, B minor, D major
8. Plein-chant chinois, Scherzo, A minor
9. Un cauchemar, E major
10. Valse boiteuse, D♭ major
11. Une pensée à Florence, A minor
12. Marche, C major

VOL.VIII ALBUM DE CHÂTEAU

1. Spécimen de l'ancien régime, E♭ major
2. Prélude pétulant rococo, G majo
3. Un regret; Un espoir, E major
4. Boléro tartare, A minor
5. Prélude prétentieux, C minor
6. Spécimen de mon temps, A♭ major
7. Valse anti-dansante, F major
8. Prélude semipastorale, A major
9. Tarantelle pour sang (avec Traversée de la procession), B minor
10. Un rêve, B minor
11. Prélude soi-disant dramatique, F# major
12. Spécimen de l'avenir, E♭ major

VOL.IX

1. Mélodie candide, A major
2. Chansonette, E♭ major
3. La savoie aimante, A minor
4. Un mot à Paganini, élégie, D major
5. Impromptu tarantellisé, F major
6. Echantillon du chant de Noël à l'italienne, E♭ major
7. Marche et reminiscences pour mon dernier voyage, A♭ major
8. Prélude, thème et variations, E major
9. Prélude italien, A♭ major
10. Une larme, A minor
11. Echantillon de blague mélodique sur les noires de la main droite, G♭ major
12. Petite fanfare à quatre mains, E♭ major

VOL.X MISCELLANÉE POUR PIANO

1. Prélude blagueur, A minor
2. Des tritons s'il vous plaît (montée-descente), C major
3. Petite pensée, E♭ major
4. Une bagatelle, E♭ major
5. Mélodie italienne: une bagatelle ('In nomine Patris'), A♭ major
6. Petite caprice (style Offenbach), C major

VOL.XI MISCELLANÉE DE MUSIQUE VOCALE

1. Ariette villageoise ('Que le jour me dure')
2. La chanson du bébé ('Maman, le gros Bébé t'appelle')
3. Amour sans espoir, Tirana all'espagnole rossinizé,
('Faut-il gémir d'amour sans retour')
4. A ma belle mère, Requiem eternam
5. O salutaris, de campagne
6. Aragonese ('Mi lagnerò tacendo')
7. Arietta all'antica, dedotta dal O salutaris ostia
('Mi lagnerò tacendo')
8. Il candore in fuga
9. Salve amabilis Maria, motet
10. Giovanna d'Arco, cantata

VOL.XII QUELQUES RIENS POUR ALBUM

24 pieces for piano.

VOL.XIII MUSIQUE ANODINE

Prélude and six petites mélodies, settings of 'Mi larnerò tacendo'.

OTHER LATE WORKS

Canone perpetuo per quattro soprani

Canone antisavant

La vénitienne, Canzonetta, C major

Deux nouvelles compositions:

1. *À Grenade* ('La nuit règne à Grenade')
2. *La veuve andalouse* ('Toi pour jamais')

Une réjouissance, A minor

Encore un peu de blague, C major

Tourniquet sur la gamme chromatique, ascendante et déscendante, C major

Ritournelle gothique, C major

Un rien (pour album) ('Ave Maria')

Sogna il guerrier (pour album)

Brindisi ('Del fanciullo il primo canto'), B major

Solo for Violoncello, A minor

Questo palpito soave

L'ultimo pensiero ('Patria, consorti, fogli!')

VOCAL EXERCISES, CADENZAS

Gorgheggi e solfeggi (1822–7)

*15 Petits exercices pour égaliser les sons, prolonger la respiration et donner
de l'élasticité aux poumons* (1858)

Petit gargouillement (1867)

SPURIOUSLY ATTRIBUTED WORKS

Duetto buffo di due gatti

Sinfonia di Odense

These recordings are all available at the time of writing. The works are listed first, followed by details of the recording: the artists, record company and disc number. All numbers given are those that apply to the compact disc format but many recordings can also be bought on conventional tape cassette. Those suggested have been chosen from the many good ones available on the basis of personal response and experience, but need only be taken as a guide.

Opera

Armida (complete)

Gasdia, Merritt, Matteuzzi, Ford, Furlanetto, Workman, Ambrosian Opera Ch., I Solisti Veneti, Scimone.

Koch Europa Dig. 350211.

Il barbiere di Siviglia (complete)

Baltsa, Allen, Araiza, Trimarchi, Lloyd, Ambrosian Opera Ch., ASMF, Marriner.
Ph. Dig. 411 058-2(3).

Callas, Gobbi, Alva, Ollendorff, Philharmonia Ch. & Orch., Galliera.

EMI CDS7 47634-8(2).

Roberta Peters, Valletti, Merrill, Corena, Tozzi, Metropolitan Opera Ch. & Orch., Leinsdorf.

BMG/RCA GD 86505(3) [RCA 6505-2-RG].

Il barbiere di Siviglia: highlights;

La Cenerentola: highlights

Berganza, Alva, Prey, Capecchi, Ambrosian Opera Ch. or Scottish Opera Ch., LSO, Abbado.

DG Compact Classics 427 714-2(2); 427 714-4.

La Cenerentola (complete)

Baltsa, Araiza, Alaimo, Raimondi, Ambrosian Opera Ch., ASMF, Marriner.

Ph. Dig. 420 468-2(2).

Le Comte Ory (complete)

Sumi Jo, Aler, Montague, Cachemaille, Quilico, Pierotti, Lyon Opera Ch. & Orch., Gardiner.

Ph. Dig. 422 406-2(2).

La donna del lago (complete)

Ricciarelli, Valentini Terrani, Gonzalez, Rafanti, Ramey, Prague Philharmonic Ch., COE, Pollini.

Sony Dig. M2K 39311(2).

Elisabetta, Regina d'Inghilterra (complete)

Caballé, Carreras, Masterson, Creffield, Benelli, Jenkins, Ambrosian Singers, New Philharmonia Orch., Masini.

Ph. 432 453-2(2).

Ermione (complete)

Gasdia, Zimmermann, Palacio, Merritt, Matteuzzi, Alaimo, Prague Philharmonic Ch., Monte Carlo PO, Scimone. Erato/Warner Dig. 2292 45790-2(2).

Guillaume Tell (William Tell) (sung in French)

Bacquier, Caballé, Gedda, Mesplé, Hendrikx, Ambrosian Opera Ch., Royal PO, Gardelli.

EMI CMS7 69951-2(4).

L'ITALIANA IN ALGERI (complete)

Valentini Terrani, Ganzarolli, Araiza, Cologne Radio Ch., Capella Coloniensis, Ferro.

Sony Dig. M2K 39048(2).

MAOMETTO II (complete)

Anderson, Zimmermann, Palacio, Ramey, dale, Ambrosian Opera Ch., Philharmonia Orch., Scimone.

Ph. Dig. 412 148-2(3)

MOSÈ IN EGITTO (complete)

Raimondi, Anderson, Nimsgern, Palacio, Gal, Fisichella, Ambrosian Opera Ch., Philharmonia Orch., Scimone.

Ph 420 109-2(2).

OTELLO (complete)

Carreras, Von Stade, Condò, Pastine, Fisichella, Ramey, Ambrosian Singers, Philharmonia Orch., Lopez-Cobos.

Ph. 432 456-2(2)

SEMIRAMIDE (complete)

Sutherland, Horne, Rouleau, Malas, Serge, Ambrosian Opera Ch., LSO, Bonynge.

Decca 425 481-2(3).

TANCREDI (complete)

Horne, Cuberli, Palacio, Zaccaria, Di Nissa, Schuman, Ch. and Orch. of Teatro la Fenice, Weikert.

Sony M3K 39073(3).

IL VIAGGIO A REIMS (complete)

Ricciarelli, Valentini Terrni, Cuberli, Gasdia, Araiza, Gimenez, Nucci, Raimondi, Ramey, Dara, Prague Philharmonic Ch., COE, Abbado.

DG Dig. 415 498-2(2).

ZELMIRA (complete)

Gasdia, Fink, Matteuzzi, Merritt, Ambrosian Singers, I Solisti Veneti, Scimone.

Erato/Warner Dig. 2292 45419-2(2).

COLLECTIONS

Arias: LA CENERENTOLA: Non più mesta. LA DONNA DEL LAGO: Mura felici … Elena! O tu, che chiamo. L'ITALIANA IN ALGERI: Cruda sorte! Amor tiranno! Pronti abbiamo … Pensa alla patria. OTELLO: Deh! calma, of ciel. LA PIETRA DEL PARAGONE: Se l'Italie contrade … se per voi lo care io torno. TANCREDI: Di tanti palpiti. Stabat Mater: Fac ut portem.

Cecilia Bartoli, A. Schoenberg Ch., Vienna Volksoper Orch., Patanè.

Decca Dig. 425 430-2 425 430-4.

Arias from: La donna de lago; Elisabetta, regina d'Inghilterra; Maometto II; Le nozze di Titi e Peleo; Semiramide; Zelmira.

Cecilia Bartoli, Ch. & Orch. of Teatro la Fenice, Marin.

Decca Dig. 436 075-2; 435 075-4.

Orchestral Works

La boutique fantasque (ballet, arr. Respighi): Complete

Toronto Symphony Orch, Davis.

Sony Dig. MDK 46508.

La boutique fantasque: Suite

ASMF, Marriner.

Ph. Dig. 420 485-2.

INTRODUCTION, THEME AND VARIATIONS IN C MINOR FOR
CLARINET AND ORCHESTRA

Emma Johnson, ECO, Groves.

ASV Dig. CDDCA 559.

OVERTURES: ARMIDA, IL BARBIERE DI SIVIGLIA; BIANCA E
FALIERO; LA CAMBIALE DI MATRIMONIO; LA CENERENTOLA;
DEMETRIO E POBLIBIO; EDIPO A COLONO; EDOARDO E CRISTINA;
[1]ERMIONE; LA GAZZA LADRA; L'INGANNO FELICE; L'ITALIANA IN
ALGERI; MAOMETTO II; OTELLO; [1]RICCIARDO E ZORAIDE; LA
SCALA DI SETA; SEMIRAMIDE; LE SIEGE DE CORINTHE; IL SIGNOR
BRUSCHINO; TANCREDI; IL TURCO IN ITALIA; TORVALDO E
DORLISKA; IL VIAGGIO A REIMS; WILLIAM TELL. SINFONIA AL
CONVENTELLO; SINFONIA DI BOLOGNA.

ASMF, Marriner, [1]with Ambrosian Singers.

Ph. 434 016-2(3).

Overtures: Il barbiere di Siviglia; La Cenerentola; La gazza ladra; L'Italiana in Algeri; Le Siège de Corinthe; Il Signor Bruschino.

LSO, Abbado.

DG 419 869-2; 419 869-4.

Overtures: Il barbiere di Siviglia; La Cenerentola; La gazza ladra; La scala di seta; Il Signor Bruschino; William Tell.

Chicago Symphony Orch, Fritz Reiner.

BMG/RCA GD 60387 [60387-2-RG].

Overtures: Il barbiere di Siviglia; La gazza ladra; L'Italiana in Algeri; La scala di seta.

Berlin PO, Karajan.

DG 429 164-2.

Overtures: Il barbiere di Siviglia; La gazza ladra; L'Italiana in Algeri; La scala di seta; Il Signor Bruschino; Semiramide; William Tell.

London Classical Players, Norrington.

EMI Dig. CDC7 54091-2.

String Sontatas

String sonatas Nos. 1–6 (complete)

Orch. of Age of Enlightenment (members). Hyp. Dig. CDA 66595.

String sonatas: No. 1 in G major, No. 4 in B♭ major, No. 5 in E♭ major, No. 6 in D major.

Liszt CO, János Rolla.

Teldec/Warner 9031 74788-2.

VOCAL WORKS

CANTATA: GIOVANNA D'ARCO. SONGS: 'L'âme délaissée', 'Ariette à l'ancienne', 'Beltà crudele', 'Canzonetta spagnuola (En medio a mis colores)', 'La grande coquette (Ariette pompadour)', 'La làgende de Marguerite', 'Mi lagnerò tacendo', 'Nizza', 'L'Orpheline du Tyrol (Ballade élégie)', 'La pastorella', 'La regata veneziana', 'Il risentimento', 'Il trovatore'.

Cecilia Bartoli, Charles Spencer.

Decca Dig. 430 518-2.

STABAT MATER

Field, Della Jones, A. Davies, Earle, LSO Ch., City of London Sinfonia, Hickox.

Chan. Dig. CHAN 8780; ABTD 1416.

AAM *Academy of Ancient Music*
arr. *arranged/arrangement*
ASMF *Academy of St. Martin-in-the-Fields*
attrib. *attributed*
bar. *baritone*
bc. *basso continuo*
bn. *bassoon*
c. *circa*
ch. *chorus/choir/chorale*
Chan. *Chandos*
cl. *clarinet*
CO *Chamber Orchestra*
COE *Chamber Orchestra of Europe*
comp. *composed/composition*
contr. *contralto*
db. *double bass*
DG *Deustche Grammophon*
Dig. *digital recording*
dir. *director*
ECO *English Chamber Orchestra*
ed. *editor/edited*
edn. *edition*
ens. *ensemble*
fl. *flute*
HM *Harmonia Mundi France*
hn. *horn*
hp. *harp*
hpd *harpsichord*
Hung. *Hungaroton*

instr. *instrument/instrumental*
kbd. *keyboard*
LSO *London Symphony Orchestra*
Mer. *Meridian*
mez. *mezzo-soprano*
ob. *oboe*
OCO *Orpheus Chamber Orchestra*
orch. *orchestra/orchestral/orchestrated*
org. *organ/organist*
O-L *Oiseau-Lyre*
perc. *percussion*
pf. *pianoforte*
picc. *piccolo*
PO *Philharmonic Orchestra*
qnt. *quintet*
qt. *quartet*
sop. *soprano*
str. *string*(s)
tb. *trombone*
ten. *tenor*
tpt. *trumpet*
trans. *translated/translation*
transcr. *transcribed/transcription*
unacc. *unaccompanied*
va. *viola*
var. *various/variation*
vc. *cello*
vn. *violin*

- Selected Further Reading -

Lord Derwent, *Rossini and some Forgotten Nightingales*, 1934;
mainly commentary on Rossini's circle.

Alan Kendall: *Gioacchino Rossini, The Reluctant Hero*, 1992;
contains plot summaries of popular operas.

Stendhal, *Life of Rossini*, 1824, trans. and ed. Richard N. Coe, 1957;
interesting and entertaining but useless as a biography of Rossini.

Nicholas Till, *Rossini*, 1934; good on the social background.

Francis Toye, *Rossini*, 1934; most amusing and readable of the popular biographies.

Herbert Weinstock, *Rossini, a Biography*, 1968, pbk 1987;
the standard biography in English.

On Rossini's music:
Philip Gossett, 'Rossini', *New Grove Dictionary of Music and Musicians* 1980.

- Acknowledgements -

The publishers wish to thank the following copyright holders for
their permission to reproduce illustrations supplied:

Archiv Für Kunst und Geschichte, London
Lebrecht Collection
Private Collection, Lebrecht Collection
The Mansell Collection Ltd

1. **THE BARBER OF SEVILLE, OVERTURE** 7'05"
   Academy of St Martin in the Fields/Sir Neville Marriner
   Rossini's most famous overture – which he had used twice before – has, as so often, no relation to the opera.

2. **THE BARBER OF SEVILLE, 'LARGO AL FACTOTUM'** 4'56"
   Thomas Allen, Academy of St Martin in the Fields/Sir Neville Marriner
   The explosive energy of this spirited cavatina, often sung by Rossini himself, makes it a perennial favorite for high baritones.

3. **THE BARBER OF SEVILLE, 'UN VOCE POCO FA'** 5'41"
   Agnes Baltsa, Academy of St Martin in the Fields/Sir Neville Marriner
   Words and music combine to create a witty and accurate portrait of the crafty but delightful heroine.

4. **LA CENERENTOLA, 'UNA VOLTA C'ERA UN RE'** 2'45"
   Agnes Baltsa, Academy of St Martin in the Fields/Sir Neville Marriner
   The sad, minor-key, folk-like melody, heard again later, beautifully suggests Cinderella's mood in her opening aria, as she sings of a king who chooses a wife for her goodness, not glamor.

5. La Cenerentola, 'Siete voi? Questo è un nodo avviluppato' 8'51"
Francisco Araiza, Agnes Baltsa, Felicity Palmer, Carol Malone, Simone Alaimo,
Ruggero Raimondo, Academy of St Martin in the Fields/Sir Neville Marriner
The sextet from Act II is a superb largo which marks the final transformation of the heroine
from humble maid to passionate woman.

6. La Cenerentola, 'Nacqui all'affanno e al pianto   Non più mesta' 7'25"
Agnes Baltsa, Ambrosian Opera Chorus, Academy of St Martin in the Fields/Sir
Neville Marriner
The final rondo, heard before in a different form in Il barbiere*, has plenty of fireworks but*
also contains the note of pathos which makes La Cenerentola *something more than broad comedy.*

7. Mosè in Egitto, 'Dal tuo stellato soglio' 5'07"
Ruggero Raimondi, Salvatore Fisichella, June Anderson, Sandra Browne,
Philharmonia Orchestra/Claudio Scimone
This prayer, though not included in the original version of Mosè, has always been the most
popular of choruses which provide a welcome contrast to the florid arias written for singers
such as Colbran.

8. **The Thieving Magpie, Overture** 9'54"
   Academy of St Martin in the Fields/Sir Neville Marriner
   One of Rossini's most popular overtures, and more closely related than usual to the opera that follows, it is full of fine effects, from the opening drum roll indicating soldiers returning from war to the breath-stopping Rossinian crescendo.

9. **William Tell, Overture** 11'06"
   Academy of St Martin in the Fields/Sir Neville Marriner
   This overture, often performed even in times when the opera was not, is a frankly programmatic work in four movements, full of lovely ideas, from the calm of the five opening cellos onward, and including perhaps the best of Rossini's favored horn solos.